BANISHING ALEX

BANISHING ALEX

A NOVEL

WILLIAM BLACKWOOD

Banishing Alex

© William Blackwood, 2024

For permission requests, email the author at:
williamblackwood@myyahoo.com

First Edition

This is a work of fiction. All the characters, names, incidents, organization, and dialogue in this novel are either the products of the author's imagination or are used fictionally.

ISBN: 979-8-218-43997-2

Cover Photography:
McKenna Fry

Cover Model:
Karee Stollsteimer

Cover Design:
Natasha Grey

Interior Design:
Vivian Freeman Chaffin

Printed in the United States of America

To my wife, Brenda.

*We have been married for thirty-nine years and
she is truly my other half. The life we've led has been amazing.*

I love you and look forward to the rest of our journey.

BANISHING ALEX

ONE

As a small-town attorney, I don't get many big cases. Mostly real estate transfers, divorces and drunk driving tickets. The television lawyers with high-profile murder cases and last-minute confessions by the villains just don't happen in real life.

I received a call from law school friend Mark Thomas who started out as a public defender in New York. As his career advanced, he became a circuit judge in Long Island, New York. I still think of him as the young college student who did all the regular dumb things. On our first day at college, we were assigned as roommates. I walked into our dorm room to find a six-foot-one student hanging his clothes in one of the closets. He had broad shoulders and wavy brown, shoulder-length hair. He looked like he should be on a beach with a surfboard. Not my normal social group.

He held out his hand and introduced himself as Mark Thomas. "I play basketball and tennis," he offered, trying to find some common ground. I introduced myself as Ronald Woods. My brown, short hair topped a five-foot-eight frame of a hundred ninety pounds. I was not then and am still not in any way an athlete. His size and athleticism were intimidating and I didn't think we would stay roommates for long. Our only common ground was our prelaw majors, so studying together brought us closer as friends.

Despite our differences we stayed roommates. We discovered a common love of books, murder mysteries and sci-fi novels. We played Dungeons and Dragons with a group, and competed in campus board game tournaments. Anything that required skill in planning an attack was our specialty. Mark had several chances to join a fraternity but turned them down. I could have joined one of the geek fraternities but never did. We never lost touch as friends even though our paths took different directions.

Knowing Mark as I do, it's hard to think of him as a wise, all-knowing judge. Since becoming a judge, he finds most people speak to him with reserved generic comments such as, "Looks like rain" or "How about those Mets?" He calls me once in a while just to hear a friendly voice and to have a normal conversation with another human.

This call was different. He wanted to know my normal hourly rate. "There are hundreds of lawyers in New York City. Why would you ask me to do anything?"

"Because you're the only one I know that might take on a special case I'm working with," Mark said.

I was ashamed to admit my normal hourly rate was $150. That sounds like a lot to a regular person. Big city rates are $300 to $500, but I am not in a big city. I have a small office with one assistant in a Pennsylvania town of six thousand addresses.

Mark announced, "I have a referral for you. The client is willing to pay $500 in advance for an initial consultation if you sign a confidentiality agreement before hand."

"What does the case involve?" I asked.

"Sorry, I can't say anything more until you sign the agreement."

Everyone knows what you tell your lawyer is privileged, so why the cloak and dagger approach? I reminded him I don't specialize in any particular branch of the law.

"No problem. It's a simple case, he assured." You just need to keep it quiet."

I agreed to the consultation.

He said, "The client wants a 6:00 A.M. appointment."

"I don't open until 9:00 A.M." I protested.

He insisted by reminding me a $500 advance was enough to roll me out of bed. He would overnight a cashier's check and be in touch.

The check arrived the next day along with a four-page confidentiality agreement. If I weren't a lawyer, I would have needed one to read through the document. It swore me to secrecy five different ways with a $2 million penalty if I divulged any of the confidential parts of the case. Nothing about the particulars or those involved was revealed. I was guaranteed $500 and did not have $2 million, so, I signed the agreement and sent it back. The only thing I knew about my new client was their initials, A.A.

Two days later an email from Mark showed up, requesting a meeting for A.A. the following Monday at 6:00 A.M. I noted the date on my calendar.

+——≍——+

Over the weekend I tried to figure out what this case could be. Mark had said it would be easy. But why send an easy case to me? It didn't make sense.

I came up with multiple scenarios but narrowed to two possibilities. My favorite involved a mobster's wife wanting a divorce. After years of marriage, she learned what her husband does for a living and refuses to tolerate it any longer. You would think the abundant cash flow and his coworkers not having necks would have provided a hint. Using an out-of-town attorney makes sense for the sake of discretion. Surely, my friend wouldn't involve me in a dangerous situation. Would he?.

Another scenario involved a multimillionaire needing a last will in testament made the most sense. The person probably didn't want any of the heirs to know how the estate would be split. There could be an illegitimate love child, or a mistress or multiple siblings arguing over whose share was larger. Now, that's a case I could handle. I've written hundreds of wills without one sign of danger. I just have to make sure the document is incontestable. There must be a lot of money involved with all the secrecy.

+——≍——+

Monday morning, I arrived at the office by 5:30. I put on a pot of coffee in case my $500 client wanted some. My assistant, Brenda, wasn't due until 9:00 A.M. so I would be alone with the client.

I waited in my private office with the door opened just enough to see into the reception area. At 6:00 A.M. the front door opened. A young girl entered. I waited a few minutes for an adult to follow but no one did. Was this my secret client?

Walking out to meet her, I estimated her age to be somewhere between thirteen and fifteen. She wore a long floral dress that hung down

5

to her ankles. Her hair was blond, long and straight. It was neatly pulled back into a ponytail, without streaks or highlights. Most girls have two or three different colors running through their hair. Her fingernails were clean and well groomed. No polish, glitter or manicure. Her appearance was contradictory to the usual teenage styles.

Her skin was blemish free. She looked thin but healthy. Her tan seemed natural, not over the top like from a tanning booth. She was young and feminine but well-toned and solid. With the right clothing she could pass for twelve or thirteen. I guess this isn't a divorce case.

Her hands lay clasped on her lap, and she stared at the floor. I approached her and held out my hand to introduce myself. She looked up revealing beautiful blue eyes. She was so young, shy and demure. What could I do for this child?

"Hello, I'm Ronald Woods."

She accepted my hand and stood as her gaze turned cold and her attitude changed. Looking me right in the eye, I felt as if she could see into my soul.

"My name is Alexandria Andres." Reading the response in my body language, she continued. "I use to go by the name Alex Andres."

It didn't seem possible, but her gaze intensified, sending shivers down my spine. Not knowing what else to say, I blurted out, "Glad to meet you, Alexandria."

Her shoulders dropped immediately, and the shy girl returned. Whatever she was looking for was gone. Her guard was down. I have to admit I was a little shaken, but gathered my composure and invited her into my office.

Indicating a chair, I asked, "How can I help you, Alex?" The cold eyes returned in an instance. I made a mistake, but wasn't sure how.

The hard stare softened as she said, "Please, do not call me, Alex. My name is Alexandria."

"Okay," I said, "Alexandria it is. What can I do for you?"

"I need to become an emancipated minor and change my legal name," she said.

Not what I expected, so I asked her age and about her family situation.

"I'm almost seventeen. My mother died four years ago and I never knew my father. After that I lived with my grandmother but she went into the nursing home eighteen months ago."

She explained her guardian was Jeremy Staley, a forty-year-old who had taken care of her for a year and half. She assured me he was not related to her and had no legal claim other than her grandmother signing over guardianship. She stated there was no abuse, but she wanted to cut all ties and become legally responsible for herself.

This took a minute to sink in. An obviously intelligent sixteen-year-old had thought this out and evidently had been coached by my friend Mark. "If you are emancipated you must be able to support yourself. How would you do this?"

Without a word, she opened the binder on her lap, handing me a bank statement with her name on it and a highlighted balance of $412,582.09. I tried not to gasp out loud and could tell she was watching my reaction. This girl had more money than most of the people I know.

"Did you come about this money legally?"

"Of course, I did," she exclaimed. "It's mine."

Assuming she was telling the truth, I went to my next question. "If you're being treated fairly and not being abused, why do this?"

With a slow planned sentence she said, "I just want control of my life. Can you help me and will you take my case?"

She was smart. She gave away just enough to pique my curiosity but wanted a commitment before sharing all the facts. Mark knew I loved a challenge and had coached her well. The little voice in the back of my mind screamed, *This is bad! This is very bad!* I told myself to get a grip, that I was just being paranoid. If I cannot convince a judge to grant her emancipation, how would it change my life? She had the money to try. So, I told the little voice to be quiet.

"Sure, I'll take the case."

Reaching in the bottom drawer of my desk, I pulled out the normal retainer agreement and told her we needed to discuss fees.

She sat up in her chair and once again looked me in the eyes. "I understand your normal fee is $150 per hour. I will be glad to pay that plus any travel fees and expenses you might incur. Or would you be willing to take a flat fee of $10,000 right now to make it easier?"

This had Mark's fingerprints all over it. We had played numerous mind games back in college and he was good at them. He knew I would be tempted by the guaranteed money. As hard as it was, I told her the hourly rate was the fairest for all involved but a retainer was necessary to begin my representation of her.

Without flinching, she produced a cashier's check for $10,000 in my name and laid it on the desk. Again, Mark's work. By bringing the cashier's check, she had covered all the bases. With her signature on the retainer naming me as her lawyer, she shrunk back into the chair. Once again, I saw the shy little girl that had entered my office less than an hour ago. This girl could sell ice cubes to Eskimos.

She explained preliminary work had taken place to assist in my efforts and handed me a folder from a law office in Long Island. Inside was a note from Mark.

> *Ronald, do not call the law office. Forward any questions you may have about this file or the case directly to me and only me. Good Luck. You'll need it.*

Alarms exploded in my head. My so-called friend had sent me a client, but it felt like I was being played. You know that sinking feeling when the bottom is about to drop out, but everything appears normal on the surface? Well, it was making a run from the pit of my stomach up to my throat.

Alexandria said, "You really don't know who I am, do you?"

I shook my head no.

She smiled that shy little girl's smile. "I am so glad. Judge Mark was right to send me to you. I need to make an appointment with you in one week at the same time."

I asked for her phone number, but she refused to give it to me.

"I'll be here next week at 6:00 A.M. By then we'll have plenty to discuss, I guarantee it." She was toying with me. "Do you have internet access and are you familiar with Google, Facebook or X?" she asked.

"Of course." I had used Google. I knew about Facebook but didn't have an account. I was clueless when it came to what X stood for.

"Good," she said and got up and walked out. "See you next week," was all I heard as the outer door closed.

I sat there for a minute, staring at the check while my computer booted up. What just happened? Was this good or bad? When the computer came up, I punched up Google and typed in the name Alexandria Andres. The screen filled. The more I read, the louder my gasps. *This is bad, this is very bad.*

At least I had heard of her. She had been all over the news at one point. How could I not have recognized her name? I don't know much but I recognize trouble when I see it. How could Mark think I could handle this?

I thought about ripping up the check then calling and telling her I changed my mind. Then I remembered she didn't leave a contact number. Mark again. I called his cell. No answer. I left a message that basically said I knew he was there and to pick up. Frustrated, and a little nervous, I hung up. Wow, can it be that bad? *Get a grip. I can do this.* I had a client to help.

Okay, get organized. Start from step one. Gather information. Figure out what I had and how to proceed.

Two

Searching for Alexandria Andres gave me scores of websites bearing her name and hundreds of blogs talking about her. I clicked the site that said, "Alexandria's Home." Up came a picture of Alexandria. She had long blond hair pulled back in a ponytail and wore a jump suit that made her look all of thirteen years of age. Her bright blue eyes danced for the camera. She was the picture of innocence in this photo. The website introduced Alexandria but did not give an age. A short video invited the viewer into her house. She smiled at the camera, promising to show her bedroom where she keeps all her stuffed animals and super great things. When I hit the button to proceed, a pop-up window informed me the website was part of Alexandria's Community web broadcast and I could not proceed unless I paid a membership fee.

The site didn't promise anything except a look around her house to see where she lived. Who would pay for that? A one-day membership was $1.99 or I could get a whole month for only $19.99. *What a bargain.* I was tempted to go for the monthly membership since it said I would be invited to her next special online party. I resisted, got out my credit card, followed the directions, and bought a one-day pass. As it processed, a cold chill streaked down my spine. My thoughts went to the $400K she had. Was my bank account being cleaned out as I sat waiting to see her teddy bears? The joke is on them. They should have waited until I deposited the retainer so they could steal her money back.

I realized I should keep a tally of the money spent on research. I got out a tablet and jotted down $1.99. Then beside it I wrote "Membership Fee, one day Alexandria's house." It seemed stupid but I had a feeling I should have gone with the month-long package. I hate to miss out on a good deal. If I end up needing the monthly deal to do more research, I'll feel like a fool for wasting $1.99.

Before obtaining official member status, I had to enter an email address. Of course, a special code would be sent to my email before being allowed to enter the website. *There goes my email address, too.* How many times will my address be sold? I just guaranteed myself about fifty extra emails a day.

In less than a minute the little bell on my computer dinged, alerting me I had mail. Checking Outlook, I found two new emails. The first one welcomed me to Alexandria's home and gave me the key code to the front door. *That was a cute touch.* The second one tried to sell me pills guaranteed to help with my embarrassing male problem. *A pill ordered online guarantees to help me out?* I can only imagine what kind of emails will show up by tomorrow. My little email bell went off again. *Great, I have to disable that bell.* Before I could hit the disable button it dinged again. I had not upgraded my spam software in a long time. I was sure whomever sends out those emails had long ago figured out my spam blocker. If nothing else, at least I would receive mail.

I went back to Alexandria's web page with the key code and was welcomed at the front door. After spending $1.99 for the whole day, I planned to get my money's worth and needed to thoroughly check out the site.

"Alexandria's Home" was a house set up with multiple web cameras showing the living room, dining room, kitchen, basement and foyer. You could tab through each room and see what was going on. Today there was nothing. A pop-up window stated that Alexandria was not home at the present time. No time was entered under the "She is expected to return at..." sign. I continued checking out the different rooms. It looked like a normal house with everything as it should be. A hundred twenty-nine people were logged on and watching the same nothingness as me. I have a little ADHD, but this was like watching paint dry. I felt robbed of my $1.99.

I saw the dog's food bowl in the kitchen and a box with a blanket in the living room. What breed of dog does she have? Is it male or female? Was the dog spayed or neutered? Since she's a small girl, the dog would need to be well trained if a large breed. *Wait a minute, I'm getting sucked in.* This was like a soap opera. I refocused on the buttons.

Another button claimed to give access to Alexandria's bedroom, so I clicked only to have a new pop-up message about not having access to that part of the house. Of course, I could buy the next key code to enter. *I'm seeing a pattern here.* I closed the window offering the new key code and checked the site for other offerings.

I found a chat room button that let me in at no extra cost. *My $1.99 fee hit pay dirt.* Several subscribers were engaged in a back-and-forth chat, so I started reading. Apparently, Alexandria had not been "home" for a while. Some said it had been over four months, others claimed it was only six weeks. Which was it and why the discrepancy?

Participants asked about reported sightings and were they real or a hoax. Alexandria had supposedly been sighted in almost every major city across the country. One person believed Alexandria was in drug rehab. Garnering a response from five people who immediately replied, "There's no way she's in rehab. Stop spreading false rumors." Boy they were defensive.

Another theory was that she was on vacation and would tell everyone all about it in a new video tape when she returns. The chat threads read as if they came from personal friends concerned for her well-being.

At last, I decided to enter some comments to see what kind of responses I would get. To set up my account I had to enter a screen name and decided on John Doe. Since there were twenty-eight other John Does, I became JOHN DOE 29. I typed, "I'm new to Alexandria's Home. Can someone tell me about her?" I was treated like a long-lost relative.

The chat line lit up. Short liners wrote, "What do you want to know?" and "Glad to meet you." These were followed by long paragraphs from those fans who considered her a close friend. They were concerned about where she was and what she was doing.

Most subscribers talked about what a clean wholesome girl she was. She was beautiful, smart and loved talking to new friends. She received good grades and always obeyed her parents, never giving them trouble.

She has a great group of friends that came over to play games and watch movies. She allowed fans to see life from her point of view as they watched what she did at home and with her friends.

I wondered how these people felt about the money collected each month for the privilege of "being her friend." Only $19.99 a month, what a bargain. *What a bunch of suckers.* But I knew if I wanted them to chat with me, I better play nice.

I asked if there was a better way to get to know her and the reply was to read her story and see some of the videos. Well, I am always up for watching movies so I found the "MY Life" page and read up on Alexandria. She was thirteen when Richard Davis Enterprises chose to publicize her and her life. Instead of a reality show lasting a few months, the producers chose an online program focusing on one girl and what she did in her life for several years. Not a star's daughter. Not anyone that was already well-known. Just a normal everyday hometown girl. That is how "Alexandria's Home" began. In the small print, it stated the site was strictly for entertainment purposes and not real-life activities. Subscribers agreed to the sharing of information with other affiliate parties. *How many times will my email address be shared or sold.*

No matter how it all began, she had a huge following. At that moment, there were over a hundred paying people on the site. The unbelievable part was Alexandria had not been seen on the site between six weeks and four months. By now people should have moved on to the next greatest online fad. *These fans are devoted.*

I checked out the list of videos I could watch for my $1.99 day pass. The first was titled "Moving Day." I clicked on the start button and waited while it queued up on my monitor. My viewing screen was quickly interrupted by yet another pop-up window informing me the cost to watch was 99¢. *What was I thinking?* I only paid $1.99 for the whole day. How could I ever think that would cover videos? Once again, I got out my credit card and typed in the number. Once again, I agreed to the sharing and selling of my personal and email addresses. Wow, I missed the regular mail stipulation. That means my mailman will be getting a workout also. I thought about the post office losing money. *They need the business and I have a good shredder, bring it on.*

Since I planned to watch a few of the videos, I searched for a package discount. No such luck. I would have to fork out 99¢ for each one. I was still steaming over the monthly deal I passed up. I wondered how many people had watched this first original video at 99¢ each. No wonder she had over $400,000 in her checking account. I took out my expense pad and noted "99¢—Moving Day video." I began realizing the $10,000 payment Alexandria offered for everything might not have been such a good deal. Almost forgetting to jot down my start time for billing purposes, I grabbed another pad and a cup of coffee.

THREE

The words "Moving Day" in giant pink letters displayed across the screen then the camera panned back and forth in front of a two-story home. The view from the road revealed a typical suburban neighborhood. The house had an average-sized front yard encircled by a white picket fence. A bird bath set in the middle of a small rock garden and a flagpole with an American flag stood amid recently cut and well-groomed grass. Burgundy shutters framed the windows and a burgundy front door accentuated the house covered in white vinyl siding with an attached two-car garage. A glimpse of the neighbors' homes confirmed they were similar in size and design. I had driven by thousands of homes in neighborhoods just like this one. It could be in any town in America. The only indication of location was the address on the mailbox, "1 Andres Way." Not much of a clue but it made sense.

The camera moved from the front to the side to a backyard enclosed by a chain link fence. A swing set meant for older kids occupied part of the backyard. Constructed from four-by-four posts and heavy chains attached to the seats, it reminded me of what you would see in a park or a grade school playground. There was plenty of grass at the back of the yard for play or for a dog to run around. A wooden fence across the back of the property offered a mere semblance of privacy. Neighbors resided in back and on both sides. As the camera rested on the backside of Alexandria's house you could see a screened back patio. Nothing out of the ordinary. Just a typical white-collar home. I paused the video to think about the house.

What kind of a job did Alexandria's father have? Maybe he was also an attorney. I wondered about the payment on a house like that and could I afford it? Maybe he was a business owner, possibly a schoolteacher. The house was nice so he must be earning an above average wage. *Wait a minute.* What am I doing? I am getting sucked into the story again. I only have access to this site for one day and I'm wasting my time. Maybe I needed to buy the monthly access deal. There goes the $1.99.

I started the video again. It focused on the front door then the camera turned toward the driveway showing more houses across the street. After a few seconds, a big red moving truck pulled up in front of the house. A van painted the same color pulled into the driveway. The camera zoomed in to the driver's door which read "Rick's Moving Crew." Out of the truck and van popped six women. Some were dressed in partially unzipped workman's coveralls while others wore bib overalls. The cleavage was front and center. *This was not a typical moving crew.* Who would move the washer and dryer and dressers and other monstrous items? Where was the fat guy who would bend over and show his butt crack several times? I bet no one in this crew was named Bubba. The video wasn't realistic but the idea was to entice people to pay to watch. A video with sexy women getting all hot and sweaty while moving furniture attracts a certain type of viewer. The paying kind.

The next few minutes concentrated on the women stretching and bending to warm up their muscles for all the work ahead. Again, to the benefit of a paying audience. After a sufficient warm-up they lifted the back door of the truck, revealing a truckload of furniture. Almost on cue, a car with four guys pulled up in an open convertible and parked behind the moving truck. The guys appeared to be around twenty years old, tan and muscular. They must have been on their way to the basketball court to shoot some hoops because they were all wearing shorts and shirts cut just above their six-pack abs. Whether you prefer men or women the person filming the video made sure there was someone for everyone. It was all about getting people to pay the price to watch.

The guys jumped out of the car without using the doors and the driver walked up to the female crew and said, "Hey, my name is Jesse. My boys and I need a good workout. Do you need any help?" The women all smiled and nodded yes. Being a lawyer, the only thing crossing my mind was worker's compensation. What would happen if one of these guys got hurt on the job? Rick, the owner, could lose everything. I know it was a dumb thought. This was all a video just for entertainment.

No other names were mentioned. In fact, they didn't say anything intelligible. They were talking and laughing amongst themselves, but the viewer was unable to hear their conversations. Music from the car stereo blared as they worked. Why didn't they say their names? We should know their names. I started to make up names for them. Once again, I had to tell myself to get a grip.

Over the next hour, the ten-person crew moved things from the back of the truck to the front door but as they went into the house the camera lens returned to the truck. Pulsating muscles, sweaty arms and backsides were the prevalent closeup shots. A water fight broke out during a rest break and wouldn't you know it, some of the girls got their front sides soaked. The cameraman earned his pay, making sure he got the money shots that would bring in the viewers without anyone taking off their clothes. As the couch was carried in, one of the girls patted the cushions to test how firm they were. Her strokes across the leather padding were captured on tape, almost crossing the line of indecency if you choose to look at it that way. Otherwise, it was just a normal moving crew minus the fat guy.

All of a sudden, the truck was empty, and they all stood around and smiled at each other. The last shot was of the ten-member moving crew going into the house they had just furnished. I figured they all needed to use the bathroom.

I perused the other video choices. They were set up in chronological order so you could start from the beginning and not miss any part of the story. There were about fifteen videos to choose from. If they all lasted an hour, I would have some serious time booked under background research. I decided to limit myself to just a couple to figure out which ones would give me the best chance of getting to know Alexandria's story.

As tempting as it was the one marked "Alexandria Gets a Dog" was not going to make the short list of must see. Once again, I started wondering what kind of a dog she had. How do you pick the right breed for such a show? Do you go to the local dog pound or buy a special one? There is no way I can justify charging my client time to view that video. I could watch the video and not charge the client for the time. *Wow, this is addicting.* Now I was thinking of spending my own time and money just to see a stupid dog in a video.

Another tempting headline was "Alexandria Gets a Tree House." Now, I know what the extra space in the backyard would be used for. Without watching the construction of the tree house, I already knew Rick's construction crew would likely get the job and the odds are they look a lot like Rick's moving crew. How many people watched the tree house being built and how many watched to see the crew building it? I passed on that one as well.

I settled on "Alexandria's First Night." The idea behind the videos became clear. Information about her was being doled out in bits and pieces with each video, requiring payment to watch. The introductory video that told her story would not bring in the desired revenue. The $400K came from many, many viewers who watched and learned from the videos. When I had asked about her using the online chat the responses directed me to the videos. I guess if they paid the price, I should too. In my case, I was going to bill it back anyway, but I wanted to be careful with my time and her money.

I hit the view video button under the "House Tour" video and was told I would have to pay an extra fee. No surprise there. Here goes another 99¢. Pressing the "continue" button brought up the increased price of $1.99 to view this video. How could people spend that kind of money on this? But I guess the $400,000 had to come from somewhere. Since I'm pretty tight with my money it was really hard to press the payment button, but reluctantly did so and was immediately asked if the credit card on file was my preferred payment method. I pushed the accept button and sighed, knowing my card was getting hit again. I immediately took out my expense pad and wrote down "$1.99 house tour video."

As my computer loaded the show, I took out a note pad to jot things down I might need to ask about. The video began with the front exterior, panning the surrounding neighborhood. This appeared to be the same as in "Moving Day and wondered if I had purchased a rerun.

After a few passes the camera pointed down the road as a black Jeep Grand Cherokee stopped in front of the house. Finally, I would learn a little about this girl.

A woman got out of the driver's side door and walked around the vehicle, stopping on the sidewalk. She stood about five-foot-eight. She had bleached blond hair and blue eyes, was well built and appeared to be in her early thirties. Her beautiful smile beamed at the camera displaying perfectly straight white teeth as she announced being Alexandria's mother. Her opening monologue gave her name as Ann Andres. She would be giving the house tour today.

She wore form fitting jeans that showed off her shape without being too tight. The name on her designer top was unrecognizable but looked expensive. Stretched to its limit, the top revealed her figure but did not expose anything. The attire was chosen to portray a clean wholesome appearance. The perfect mother for the perfect girl.

Ann explained the house was in a nice neighborhood and they were lucky to have found the ten-year-old, four-bedroom house. The school was a mile away and a mall was two miles to the south, adding to the location's appeal. The camera followed her around the front and side yards of the house and eventually to the back. So far, I had not seen anything new except the Jeep and the mother.

Finally, we entered the front door, walked through a normal entryway and had a view of the living room. Not sure what I expected but was a little disappointed in the average middle-class decor. A leather sectional rested against two walls. A gas fireplace across the room was topped with a large flat screen television with a lazy boy chair positioned within comfortable viewing range. A few end tables completed the room. Everything was neat and clean surrounded by neutral colored walls. Anyone producing a home renovation show would be happy with the set up.

The dining room and kitchen were up-to-date with new appliances and countertops, but nothing out of the ordinary. A mudroom with a washer and dryer led to the garage, which was empty although there was plenty of room for two cars.

Ann's tour took us into the large master bedroom with the normal bed, dresser and nightstands. A nice cedar chest with a padded top was placed at the foot of the bed. I figured it was a good place to sit as you dressed. Again, I found myself pondering the price range of the house. Two doors opened to reveal the master bathroom and a huge walk-in closet. The bathroom was given a cursory sweep by the camera. The closet held the usual clothing items, but the camera lingered on various styles of women's lingerie draped on satin hangers.

The family room was large and comfortably furnished with a couch and television hooked up to an Xbox 360 and Wii Fitness on one side of the room, while a treadmill and a stationary bicycle as well as some weights were staged on the opposite side. I wondered if Ann's work-out program had been recorded. If people are paying just to look at a normal house, I'm sure they would subscribe to watch a beautiful woman going through her exercise routine.

As we followed our guide up the stairs to a landing area, I realized the camera focused on Ann's backside. I took no offense following behind her, but it was too convenient for the camera to stay in the same position all the way up. A little sexual innuendo was added for the viewers. Ann explained to her audience she was in the middle of remodeling the three upstairs bedrooms and bath into a second master bedroom with connecting bath and an office. The camera followed her back down the stairs to the front door where she thanked us for coming on the tour. The video was over.

I felt robbed as I realized I had not written anything on the pad under "Important things I had seen." By not showing Alexandria's bedroom and by telling us it was under construction they guaranteed two more videos, one with Rick's construction crew and another showcasing Alexandria's bedroom. My tour of the house gave me little information plus I lost another $1.99 and twenty minutes of my life. Thank goodness we agreed on billing by the hour instead of a flat fee.

Four

As I sat at my desk pondering the wasted money and time, I heard the front door open and the shuffling noise of my office assistant settling in at her desk. Juggling work and a home life, Brenda is in her mid-forties with a husband and two daughters. She has been with me for over ten years and regardless of her official title, we both know she runs the office. I walked out to update her on our new client.

Brenda's area was located off the front door lobby. Nobody reaches me without checking with her first. Our furniture has seen better days. The worn places on her wooden desk revealed where previous calendars and day planners sat in years past. Those things are long gone having given way to computers. Plans for the day are right on the screen when I sit down in the morning. In the past we had a ten-minute meeting to discuss the day's schedule. Truth is, I miss those days.

My office at the rear of our three-room suite also holds a wooden desk. One that's too old to be considered modern but too new to be vintage. If it is humid outside the bottom right-hand drawer sticks almost to the point of not being able to open it. Nothing important can be stored in that drawer. The only other room beside the bathroom is a conference room with a large table that will accommodate ten people, although I don't remember ever having more than four at one time. All the walls are brown paneling. *It might be time for some remodeling.* After all, it is 2023. This office looks straight out of the 1980s.

I called Brenda into my office. "Have a seat. A new client signed on with us this morning. The referral came from Mark Thomas."

Brenda grabbed a pen and began jotting down pertinent information on a legal pad.

"The case involves a high-profile celebrity seeking to be emancipated and change her name. I'm still not sure of this person's ultimate goal other than those two legal aspects. This case also involves a high-degree of confidentiality. So much so that the confidentiality agreement listed a $2 million penalty if any information leaks from this office." It wasn't that I didn't trust my assistant, but the stakes are high and I couldn't take the chance of anything being misunderstood.

"Are you going to tell me who this new client is or am I supposed to guess?" Brenda asked.

"Her name is Alexandria Andres. Have you heard of her?"

Brenda's face changed from its cheerful natural blush to almost ashen as she visibly swallowed hard. "What were you thinking?"

It was true that I really didn't know much about the online celebrity. "Alexandria seemed like a nice young girl," I said. "Besides, she's only sixteen and needs our help."

Brenda explained to me that representing Alexandria Andres was only half the job. "You'll also represent Alex Andres."

"She did get a little defensive when I called her Alex during our meeting this morning." It was obvious I still hadn't grasped the full situation.

Brenda proceeded to fill in the blanks. "Alexandria first appeared online about three years ago. The original idea, as I understand it, was to follow a normal teenage girl around for a few years and see life through her eyes. With her All-American look, people flocked to her site as she smiled and welcomed them and their credit card numbers. As the weeks progressed, it became apparent two kinds of viewers were subscribing to the website. One wanted to follow the wholesome girl next door and the creeper crowd, who wanted to watch a little girl. The producer was only interested in the money and didn't want to lose either group, so he created Alexandria and Alex. One girl leading two distinctively different lives. It worked like a charm.

"Supporters of Alexandria hate the fact that their perfect little girl is forced to play the role of Alex and has to act that way. They've requested the Alex cameras be shut down because their little miss sunshine would never act or dress that way. The Alex supporters don't care whether she plays the Alexandria part, expecting she will eventually turn to the dark side. After all, they are only in it to watch the smutty parts of the videos. On the business side the producers get rich playing both sides of the street."

It suddenly dawned on me that my client plans to ditch one of the characters she portrays. "From what I witnessed in my office this morning, she's ditching the Alex character," I said, "which will anger half of her viewers and cost producers a large portion of their income. This will be a fight."

Brenda raised an eyebrow in my direction, signaling both her agreement with my statement and her dismay with me for accepting such an explosive case. She returned to her desk shaking her head as she relayed one last thought. "Let me know when the trouble starts."

Walking away from such a huge viewing audience would be hard to do. Everyone on the Alexandria website truly wanted to know where she was, what she was doing and most of all that she was safe. The Alex crowd probably spent twice as much time and money trying to track her down, but their obsession was of a different nature. Huge blocks of television coverage had focused on finding her over the last four months. There's almost no place she could hide without being recognized. Any fan with a cell phone would have uploaded her photo and location to Facebook the moment she was seen, allowing her to be tracked by everyone.

How had she done it? Why come back now? Maybe she just wants to get rid of Alex and continue playing Alexandria. Her ultimate goal would be part of our next discussion.

No wonder Mark had sent her to me and requested a 6:00 A.M. appointment. This small town had pretty much forgotten about her. She had slipped in and out without being seen. The day I file papers in court on her behalf my firm's name and address will be public and I'll be inundated with reporters and detectives. Not being able to contact her at this point was a good thing. The only ones who knew anything were Mark and my assistant, Brenda.

I knew Brenda was a safe bet to keep quiet and Mark had sent her to me. Everything could be kept in check for at least a week. My adrenalin flowed as the steps of how to proceed began developing in my mind. On one hand I enjoyed my peaceful life but the challenges of this case excited the kid in me. Could I really represent such a notable client?

Then there was Mark. The thought of my friend sending this case to me sent two waves of emotions. The first was the potential size of the case, certainly assuring television and internet appearances. How this would affect my practice and my future is a guess at this stage, but it would be life changing to say the least. I wanted to email Mark and thank him. The second wave came as I grasped the expectation of television and internet. My life as I knew it would be over. That realization was so strong I found myself swallowing hard to avoid throwing up. At that very moment I wanted nothing more than to kill Mark for putting me in this position.

<hr />

Technically, the aspects of the case were simple. Being a minor, any contracts she had entered into could be made null and void. Her emancipation would be the first step. The name change comes second. Maybe it would give her a fresh start. In a normal situation these two steps are not that difficult. If no one fights the request, it goes smoothly. However, this was not a normal situation with thousands, perhaps millions of dollars at stake. A court fight was almost guaranteed.

My fees will likely add up to a lot. This could get ugly if her guardian doesn't agree to release his golden goose. If she has over $400K in her bank account, how much had the investors made? If they want to fight it, the court battle could be a long one.

I had to swallow hard again when I thought of the purposed $10,000 flat fee I almost accepted. Was the flat fee offer some kind of test to see if I would go for the easy money then take advantage of a young client? Visualizing Mark smiling at the mind game he had played bothered me and the worst part was it had worked. I need to forget his strange sense of humor and concentrate on the case.

How could I get a feel for the Alex crowd? I had already formed my own opinion of them and needed to avoid prejudgment. A Google search for Alex Andres landed a mega list of hits. The top one invited me to Alex's house. This was like *déjà vu*. I could feel my credit card preparing for another work out. Nothing on this site would be free and likely added me to some kind of sex offender list just for going to the site. I got out my credit card and apologized knowing it was a virgin to these sites.

I decided to take the plunge and hit the listing for "Alex's House." The screen lit up and there she was. It was the same girl but with a totally different appearance. Instead of blond hair, it was bright red and hung almost to her waist. The sleeves had been ripped from her button up shirt, which was tied above the waist, exposing her midsection. Cut off jean shorts rode high on her backside, exposing some of her butt cheek. She wore lipstick and heavy, dark eye shadow. Giant hoop earrings hanging from both ears and a tattoo etched on her upper right arm completed the ensemble.

Alex did not look like the girl in my office who could have passed for thirteen. This girl didn't look twenty-one, but she looked old enough to sneak inside a biker bar. What a difference environment can make on your appearance and how you develop. The viewer decided which girl and lifestyle they preferred to watch. The situations experienced and how those were handled would be different for each girl. This was a two for one deal for the producers.

I slowly stroked my credit card and realized I needed a second bank account. I've heard about people keeping separate accounts with separate debit cards to reduce the risk of having their main account cleaned out through illegal means. The second account takes care of all your online payments so you can regulate what an online hacker can access. Keeping small balances in that account would significantly cut my losses if and when someone decided to wipe me out. *Who was I kidding?* No way would I take the time keep up with two accounts, plus I had already put my account information on the other website. If cyber thieves want my information, it's there for the taking.

We are all at their mercy, handing out our debit card at every convenience store and restaurant we visit. The sad part is that most of the time the workers at these places often look like the people you see on *America's Most Wanted*. We believe since they work at the local mall or the neighborhood quick stop, they must be okay. The worst thing we do is go online and type in our account number to buy a cheap piece of jewelry or the latest fitness video then wonder how someone ripped off our bank account.

Since signing up on Alexandria's site, twenty emails arrived in my inbox from people claiming I won a lottery or they're willing to split some vast fortune if I help them get it out of the country. Both scams require giving your bank account information so they can *safely* wire you the money, and just like that, your bank account is cleaned out. The thieves will even tack on a processing fee and people still fall for it. Once they realize the money is gone, the victims call me, begging for my help to get their money back. My first question is, "Back from where?" Since they don't know where their money went, I don't know who to go after or where to look. It is always a sad story, but what can I do?

I decided to put the case out of my mind until Monday. All I could accomplish was adding more worry to my already worried mind. I told Brenda I was waiting to hear from the client before proceeding with anything else. Surprisingly, she didn't question me about the case and continued with her daily routine.

FIVE

I arrived Monday at 5:45 A.M. Alexandria was coming in at 6:00 A.M., so I didn't have to be there any sooner. This time I wasn't making coffee or doing anything extra until I really knew what was going on. I fired up my ten-year-old computer and took a quick inventory of my office. Perhaps, after this case is resolved, I can afford to fix it up a bit. It was small and missed the attributes a client might expect. Most law offices have large reception rooms with flat screen TVs and fancy coffee makers. I had a few old paintings and year-old magazines stacked on a coffee table sitting among a few chairs with a thrift shop floor lamp in the corner. Although it was a little depressing, we were comfortable and managed to complete the work needed. *When had I gotten into this rut.* I was reminded of the song that said, "Life goes on; long after the thrill of living is gone." I could not remember the last time I did something really fun or outside the box. Maybe I would try someplace different for lunch just to shake things up. *Lame...but...baby steps.*

At 6:00 A.M. sharp the front door opened. This time I didn't wait and stepped out to meet her. There she sat again wearing a long dress down to her ankles, but today her hair was pulled into a bun at the back of her head. Hands in her lap, her head down.

When I approached, she stood and I thrust my hand forward. I had mentally rehearsed this second meeting. Then we shook and she looked me straight in the eyes and said, "I am so glad you agreed to take my case. Judge Mark assured me you were the only one he trusted with this."

My heart melted in an instant. I choked out something about being glad to see her again. I turned and she followed me into my office. She took the same chair as last week and I sat down at my desk.

"Well," she said, "I hope your opinion of me isn't too bad. I've treated people terribly in the past and want to assure you all that's behind me now. I want a fresh start. I'm sure you have a lot of questions, but I was told to give you this before we get into any details." She handed me an envelope with my name on the front. I opened it and saw Mark's letterhead. I swallowed hard to stall the sinking feeling wanting to rise from my gut.

> Ronald, you are NOT being played by Alex. Alexandria is a real girl who needs your help. We have to be extremely careful with this case or we could both end up in jail. I have complete faith that you can do this.
>
> Mark

Mark's attempt of explaining I was not being played made me even more suspicious. Forget the little warning bells. Full-size sirens were blaring in my head. *Jail?* How could I go to jail? I am not very big so jail is not an option for me. He reiterated how Alexandria needed my help. He trusted me and I needed to trust him. I could no longer hide my terror.

She watched me. I needed to look up at some point but was still trying to wrap my brain around this letter. The word "jail" kept jumping back at me. I already knew I had looked at the short message too long. Maybe she didn't know how long the letter was or maybe she assumed I was a slow reader. When I looked up, she was staring straight at me.

With a note of empathy in her voice, she said, "Mark said to tell you it will be okay."

Her words only worsened my anxiety. I regrouped and forced myself into a logical thinking pattern. I took a deep breath then proceeded to tell her what I had learned over the last week, deciding to lay all the cards on the table and discuss my feeling of representing Alex. I wanted to be sure she understood I would not be played. I needed to know exactly the end result she wanted. There must be lots of attorneys who would love to get their hands on this case and wondered how I could convince her that someone else should represent her.

She handed over another envelope with my name on it. Once again it was from Mark. It read:

This is for real. You are not being played by Alex
Alexandria needs you.

What is with these letters? This was crazy.

I realized my hand was trembling and braced it against the desk. "When did Mark write this?"

"Four weeks ago," she said.

"That was before we had even met." *Forget Alex,* I thought, *Mark is the one playing me.* I sat there thinking about my next move when she stated that she wanted to prove she had changed. This also had Mark's fingerprints on it.

"To show you I'm sincere, I want to make amends with a girl that I, in my role as Alex, bullied and harassed." Alexandria handed me a check for $250,000 made out to my escrow account.

I gasped as I read the amount.

"It's for the girl in the Sonic videos. Please make sure she gets it." Handing me a sealed envelope, Alexandria continued. "I also wrote her a letter asking for forgiveness." She then passed along another check for $150,000, also made out to my escrow account. This one for an anti-bullying charity.

I was shocked and quickly ran the numbers in my head. Checks for $250,000, $150,000, plus my $10,000 retainer and $500 for last week's consultation didn't leave much of the $412,000 balance she showed me last week. "What if legal fees go beyond the retainer. You still have to show the means to support yourself to be granted emancipation," I asked.

She didn't respond but smiled and handed me a third envelope. Instead of another letter from Mark, I found a new bank statement revealing a balance of $763,812.13. My jaw dropped. While I couldn't stop staring, first at the statement then at her, she explained the first statement was for Alexandria. I quickly glanced and noticed ALEX Andres listed at the top. All those credit cards being hit each month; all those videos being watched; all the advertisers paying to be affiliated with her site proved the Alex crowd really was obsessed with her. How much money had the producers gotten?

"I plan to give away all the money from Alex's account by the end of my case," she explained.

These two checks convinced me Alexandria was truly trying to make amends. Giving away three-quarters of a million dollars was pretty convincing. Not too many teenagers would give up that kind of money. From that point forward I was committed to representing her. I was on an out-of-control merry-go-around that was too thrilling to resist.

I looked her right in the eyes. "I'm your man. I am with you all the way."

Alexandria looked down and wiped a few tears from her cheek. "You and Mark are the only two people who really care about me other than my new family. Thank you so much."

I realized I had just committed to helping her and still didn't have all the details of her actual end goal. All of the sudden what she said sank in. *What new family?* She said she had no one. The bells and whistles clanged louder. The part Mark mentioned about possible jail time had also slipped from my brain. I was all in but had no idea what I was in for.

To add insult to injury she handed me one more note from Mark that read, "Welcome to the team, we are going to need you." I looked at her and asked if she had any more surprise letters from Mark.

"Not today," she said.

Her response didn't make me feel any better, because it left open the possibility of there being more in the future. *Played again, but also happy to be on the team.*

Steadying myself, I asked point blank what she expected at the end of what appeared to be an upcoming court case. She explained the goal really was to become emancipated and to change her name to achieve a fresh start away from both characters.

I had pretty much pieced together how the business worked, but I needed to know how it started. "How and when did you meet Jeremy Staley?"

Her hands returned to their relaxed position on her lap and she held my gaze and shared her story. "My grandmother was given guardianship of me when I was twelve, after my mother died. A few months later she began showing signs of dementia, so basically, I've been on my own ever since."

She explained, "Mother wasn't very good at keeping a job or anything since she was a heavy drinker. Staying with my grandmother even before Mother died was something I had done since birth."

So, her mother had died young and she had stayed with her grandmother. That explained her real home life but did not lead me to an online internet star. I guess sometimes fate just puts you in the right place at the right time. "Sorry about your mother. When did Jeremy come along?"

"I used to hang out at the local YMCA since it was close to home. My grandmother was considered low-income so I got a free membership. It was a safe place to swim and see some of my friends. They had some cool activities and grandmother let me come and go whenever I wanted. It was good.

"One Saturday afternoon they had a Karaoke event for teenagers and I liked to sing. Not many people showed up, but there were a few adults watching their kids perform. When it was your turn, you had to state your name and could tell a little about yourself. I went for the sympathy vote by telling the crowd about my mother dying, living with my elderly grandmother and that my dream was to become a singing star. At the end of the session the crowd was supposed to vote on the best singer with the winner receiving a $25 gift card. That was big money for me back then."

Was I another sympathy vote? I wondered as I noted a few details on my legal pad.

"I'm not a great singer but I tried my best with 'Stand by Your Man.' It was a song my mother played a lot although she never really had a man for very long. We got to sing a second song, so I attempted 'This Is What Dreams Are Made Of.' I stumbled through both songs and was so nervous I just about peed in my pants. A girl named Natasha did a good job with a religious song and I thought she would win, but in the end some other girl sang 'All I Want for Christmas Is You' with an upbeat tempo. She was dressed in a slinky red outfit that was way too short for a thirteen-year-old, but she showed what she had. She sang well but I think the dress put her over the top."

So, the slutty girl won, I thought.

Alexandria paused for a moment as if deep in thought.

"Go on," I said. "It's just us and I need to know everything in order to represent you."

She smiled slightly and continued. "After the contest, Jeremy came up to me and asked if I came here often. I told him almost every day after school, then I went home and didn't think anything else of it. About a week later he came back and wanted to talk to me. He had a lady with him, so I thought he was okay. We went into one of the craft rooms and sat down. He asked about my parents and I told him I lived with my grandmother. Now, I understand he was just trying to figure out how I was raised and what type of supervision I had. The answer was not much. I got good grades in school but didn't participate in sports or other activities. I had no religious background. I knew what church was but was never inside one. My only contact with church goers was around Christmas when they dropped off a few toys or some food. They never came by other than Christmas. I guess they thought we had enough to eat during the rest of the year. I have no other family so I pretty much raised myself.

"The lady said I was the perfect candidate for Jeremy's story because I didn't have any positive role models and had stayed out of trouble and avoided the dark side. I was middle of the road. When Jeremy asked if I still wanted to be famous, I actually thought he meant by having a singing career. Then he explained wanting to do a show about a girl growing up in a nice neighborhood with a mother and a father doing what a regular girl would do in a normal household. There would be cameras set up all through the house and people would watch from their computers. It was purely for entertainment purposes, and he didn't know if the program would become popular or not."

Alexandria seemed to be on a slippery slope, so I asked, "What were you supposed to do in front of these cameras?" Her answers could help when we got to court.

"I asked that same question," she said. "Jeremy said I would just do the normal stuff I did each day. I asked if I could sing and he told me I could do anything I wanted. To start they would have some new friends come over and stay the night like a slumber party. We would take trips to stores and shop. My new internet mother would take me out to eat and all kinds of things. I thought it was kind of stupid for people to watch me, but he explained this was just a trial and he didn't know how long it would last. If people liked watching, it could turn into a long-term show."

She stopped and asked, "Mr. Woods, how many thirteen-year-old kids do you think would turn down a chance to have an internet show and possibly become famous?"

"Probably not many," I answered.

Alexandria nodded and continued. "I had nothing to lose and agreed to do a pilot, although no one knew how it would turn out. Because I wanted to try it, my grandmother agreed. She had her attorney negotiate the terms. He did a great job convincing the producers to give me ten percent of all money collected instead of a set dollar amount. Personally, I didn't have any money anyways, so it didn't matter to me. The producer thought it was a great idea. If it flopped, I got nothing. It turned out to be a great deal for me.

"Our first show was me at home playing games on the computer and watching television. With a little promotion on social media, I had a small audience. The early shows didn't cost anything to view. They were just supposed to be fun to watch. The first pay-per-view video was advertised as a slumber party for eight thirteen-year-old girls. Radar antennas for the creeper crowd were raised and the show was a huge success. It quickly became evident that certain people were willing to pay money to watch a bunch of girls playing games in their pjs. I am not sure anyone had any idea how big this thing would get. The speed at which I gained new viewers was amazing. It seemed everyone had their own reasons for watching, so Jeremy decided to do two shows—one good girl and one bad girl. He determined if we gave both crowds more of what they wanted, they were more likely to pay."

That slippery slope seemed to be getting slicker, so I had to ask her. "You mentioned the creeper crowd. Were you ever concerned about being pushed into something more?"

Alexandria didn't hesitate with her answer. "My grandmother made them put in an amendment to the contract that I would never do anything that required me to take off my clothes. She wanted to protect me from the pornographic side of the internet. The producers agreed since the contract didn't stop my coworkers from being as indecent as they wanted. Grandma probably didn't think it through far enough. The Alex site was a huge success from the beginning.

"Over the next three years the shows became astronomical hits all around the world. The sad part is I really don't have any special talents. I consider myself average in almost every category. Somehow, the producers are able to convince viewers that a picnic on the beach is worth watching. So much so that they're willing to pay to do it. At first, all the attention and the money were great, but now I realize it's all just a waste of time."

"Why do you think it's a waste of time?" I felt it important to understand her mental capacity and maturity before putting her in front of a judge and being questioned by opposing council.

"While people are watching me and my pretend friends at the bowling alley, they could be out living their own lives. Someone out there needs their help or their companionship. Instead, they just sit around watching videos. This is just a waste. I want to take the rest of my life and do something good for those around me. Not just entertain them and take their money. Guess you can say I want to be a good person."

She gazed up at the ceiling for about ten seconds and regrouped. "I'm not saying we didn't do some good in the world. While providing entertainment we also used the platform to engage with a lot of lonely people. Ann, my internet mom, has a workout class and a Pelton class twice a week. With a regular subscription you can watch at no extra charge. There is an option to join both classes through zoom so you can participate. Another feature allows for small groups of participants so friends can sign on together. Kind of a subgroup of the group. It is very popular. We leave the rooms for those people open for an hour after the classes and there are always groups in there chatting away.

"As Alexandria I took First Aid classes. After three years it has evolved into an EMT training. I could pass the test and become a certified EMT right now. A lot of my followers have already gone on to be certified."

"That's pretty amazing to motivate others into helping their communities," I interjected.

She smiled and continued. "Audience participation was also good when we did classes on origami and flower arranging. People emailed pictures of their creations to us. Some were pretty good, so we did an online exhibit. Using their first name only we showed their artwork and allowed people to comment. We had a three-minute delay so we could filter out negative comments. People loved it.

"Alexandria's Community has become a great place for people to come and hang out to see what's next." She looked at me and asked, "Do you know the show whose theme song goes something like, 'You want to go where people know your name and are always glad you came?"

The words were not exact, but close enough to recognize. It was my time to smile. "Yes, *Cheers* was the name of that show."

She nodded her head in agreement and smiled.

"I am not saying we were not making a lot of money, but we have some good things happening, too" she added.

"Alexandria reads to the kids at a local library twice a month. We were reading a series that teaches kids about real American history, so they hear the truth. It is called the Tuttle Twins Books. They make history fun, so the kids want to hear more. We give away fifty tickets to the live show and we are always turning kids away. We live stream the readings and have thousands watching sometimes. It feels great to be a positive role model.

"Whenever there is a natural disaster, we promote the Red Cross so they can get funding when they need it most. Our community is very generous."

I shook my head and said, "I did not know anything about you two weeks ago and certainly had no idea about any of this."

"Let me tell you about the one I am most proud of. We had a tragic fire in our community where a thirty-two-year-old firefighter was trapped in a building while attempting a rescue. He lost his life and left behind a wife and two young children. The Tunnel to Towers Foundation helps pay off mortgages of fallen first responders and wounded veterans. To my surprise Jeremy announced that our community would take care of our own fallen hero. He got us a URL code from Tunnel to Towers so we could send donations directly to them. They gave a special web address and our own phone line so they could track what we brought in and know where to allocate the funding. We went live and Jeremy donated the first $5,000 from his own money. The family's mortgage was over $200,000. We raised that in less than four days. Some of our people signed up for the $11 a month on-going sponsorship and to this day people are still giving under our website and URL code. Tunnel to Towers is using the excess funds to help other fallen heroes."

"You must be very proud to be making a difference," I interjected.

"Yes, I am," she replied. "But as great as it is there is an opposite side to the business that is equally bad. One show would be hard enough to do but two shows running at the same time is impossible to maintain. It's too much to handle. I need to step back and slow down. I am a changed person. I want out."

"Technically, I'm working for you, so how would you like to proceed?"

Her response was quick and to the point. "Step one is to sever all connections to the internet business. The problem is my fan base and producers are relentless. I've been away four months, and they are still looking for me. I need to disappear and not be found, if I ever expect to have a normal life"

I couldn't argue with her conclusions. Alexandria seemed to understand this would be a difficult case.

She shifted in the chair, moving her hands to the arm rests on either side as if she needed the extra support. "My status is about to change. Right now, I'm still serving time on my sentence. That ends next week when I'll be considered a run away in the eyes of the law. Anyone who helps me or hinders a police investigation can be held in contempt of court. That is why Mark sent me to you."

"Wait right there." I exclaimed. "Mark sent you here so I could be the fall guy?"

She smiled and said there would be more letters from Mark, outlining how he thinks this will go down so no one goes to jail. I leaned over and held my head in my hands, praying I misunderstood what she just said. *Mark had a plan that would get what she wanted done and not make us go to jail?* Why was I even in this? I felt a migraine coming on.

Mark had pulled off some crazy schemes in college but this was messing with our lives. Alexandria saw I was visibly shaken and tried to reassure me by stating how she really needed my help and I was her only hope of having a normal life. She also had her new family to consider and how they could be impacted. If everything went well, they would not be brought into this.

Six

I was about to jump in head first and hoped I didn't hit rock bottom. She needed help and Mark had brought her to me. I needed to know how she got to this point and what she meant about being released.

Pulling a new legal pad from my desk drawer, I sat back with pen in hand ready to take notes. "Alexandria, start with the first time you met Mark and bring me up to speed. I need to understand these conditions he set and what he expects me to do." She looked at me with the eyes of an exhausted and lost sixteen-year-old who had grown up before her time. "Before you start, would you like some water or something?"

"No thanks, Mr. Woods. I'm okay." She scooted back in her chair as if preparing to brace herself against a force she had no control over. After letting out a deep sigh, she began. "The first time I went before Judge Mark he said I was out of control and had no respect for anyone. I really was a bad person. Imagine a teenage kid with all this popularity and money. We never had much money when I was growing up so this was a huge change. I became impossible to rein in, doing whatever I wanted and didn't care about the consequences, which played right into the Alex character.

"While filming as Alex my fake friends and I rode around town in a Jeep with the top down and pulled into a Sonic for some sodas."

Trying to get as precise a picture as possible, I asked, "Were you driving?"

"No, I sat in the back behind the driver. When I received my drink,

I told the girl at the drive-thru window I didn't get enough ice. She leaned out and said she would add some more. Just to be mean, I threw the filled cup back at her, causing the soda to go all over her. We drove away.

"Like everything else, the incident was filmed and the producers decided to put it on YouTube. The video went viral within twenty-four hours. Everyone watched it. The incident began a trend of throwing food and drinks at servers and waitresses. I had started one of the biggest bullying campaigns ever and didn't even care. I was charged with assault. That's when I met Judge Mark."

"How did that go?" I asked. "This was a court appearance, correct?"

"Yes. He sentenced me to three days confinement, fined me $1,000 and ordered me to pay $15,000 in restitution to the girl I assaulted. My confinement was a weekend at a girl's juvenile detention facility. The guards and other inmates recognized me immediately and treated me like royalty. They fell all over themselves to make me feel comfortable. After three days, I reappeared before Judge Mark and smugly told him he had to do better than spending three days with my fans if he intended to punish me. He told me if I screwed up again, the consequences would be more severe. I laughed and told him to bring it on.

"Three days away stirred up a huge controversy on my websites. All Judge Mark succeeded in doing was raise my standings in the media. More people subscribed and started watching the videos. When my producer asked if I wanted to push the judge's buttons to see what might happen, I was up for it. As we saw it, his so-called punishment would keep me in the news and bump my ratings. It was a win-win for me.

"That's when I decided to repeat the soda pop gig at the same Sonic. The cameras were rolling to get the money shots. We weren't posting these on YouTube anymore. Instead, we started charging people to view them on the website. To my surprise the same girl was working the drive-thru. She looked right at me as she handed out the drinks. She tried to close the window, but I had already launched the cup filled with soda and ice. It hit her square in the front of her shirt, exploding as planned. We laughed and raced off as before.

"Thirty minutes later the police showed up at the office as expected. We kept the cameras rolling as they handed a court summons to the producers ordering me to appear in one week on the latest assault charge. We all laughed at the thought of a fine, knowing the videos would bring in a hundred times that much with the new publicity. All was going as planned."

"So, you were back in front of Judge Mark Thomas. Did this appearance go as before?" I asked and continued my note taking.

"No, far from it." Alexandria never averted her eyes and her voice remained calm. "The next week, I appeared in court dressed as Alex just to taunt Judge Mark. The bailiff read the harassment charge. Judge Mark told me I had crossed the line and allowed the prosecutor to add a menacing charge. We were astonished by the additional charge, but with checkbook in hand my guardian stood beside me ready to pay the fine and take me home. Judge Mark sentenced me to the maximum allowed, which was three years in jail to be served immediately. Jeremy and my lawyer were stunned. The guard handcuffed me and was marching me out the door when my lawyer pleaded with the judge about other alternatives. Going to jail for three years was not part of the plan. I couldn't be gone that long. As reality hit so did the tears. I would be almost twenty before getting out. My life would be over."

"I'm guessing the judge came up with a different sentence or else you wouldn't be here. What happened?" Turning the page of my legal pad, I kept writing.

"My lawyer played right into Judge Mark's plan. He asked the bailiff to bring me back up in front of him. He knew I was a big internet personality but he wanted me to understand what it's like to work for a living. The alternative was for me to go to a work camp for six months with a chance to be out in four months with good behavior. Everyone breathed a sigh of relief. I figured the time would be like those three days I had served at the girls' jail. I could do that easily. My producers could manage working around my absence for four months."

Alexandria sat back in her chair and appeared more relaxed, although her gaze was still forward. *I still believe this girl could burn holes through me.*

"The judge set forth a few rules. The biggest of which was that no one would know where I was. Not Jeremy and not my lawyer. Jeremy had to assign temp custody of me to Judge Mark for four months. He would not have any legal rights to know where I was or what I was doing. I was allowed to tell the work crew who I was but no one else. If I violated that condition, I would go to jail for three years with no chance of getting out early. He said if after four months, I had not gotten into any trouble and wanted out, he would release me.

"Judge Mark also stated that he didn't want the place where I would be detained inundated with reporters. Jeremy brought up that the guards would probably leak the fact that I was there. The judge explained if that happened, I would not be held accountable.

"With no other alternative, Jeremy and the lawyer talked and agreed to the terms. Judge Mark then looked me right in the eye and asked, 'Ms. Andres, this is your life we're bargaining here, do you agree to this amended plan? Do you truly understand the consequences if you violate my order of not revealing your identity?' He then asked something that no one else has ever asked me. 'On your word of honor will you not divulge who you are as set forth in this agreement?' I nodded my head yes but he said I had to agree verbally so the court reporter could get it on the record. I said, 'Yes.'

"With everyone agreeing to those stipulations, he explained I would be picked up within twenty-four hours and surrender to his custody for at least four months. I was told I would not need much because everything would be provided to me. Judge Mark also insisted that news of my incarceration not be leaked until three hours after I was dropped off at the work camp. Then the details of the agreement could be made public."

"How did your guardian and your attorney respond to these rules? Were they upset over the rules?"

"No, just the opposite. As we left, Jeremy and the attorney congratulated each other on how they had escaped a catastrophe and how this would become a huge moneymaker. They expected the next four months to pass quickly and the amount of publicity generated would be enormous. Jeremy instructed me to have someone leak my whereabouts so they could at least get some shots and interviews of the workers to share with my fans. He assured me there was no place Judge Mark could send me where someone would not know who I was.

"If you weren't taken into custody at that time, where did you spend that night?" I asked.

"Judge Mark said to go home and wait," she answered. "That night I kept thinking about *Holes*. The movie with the work camp where everyone had to dig everyday all day in the hot sun. That had to be the worst-case scenario. I wondered if those places really existed. If I did end up in a place like that, I knew I was young and strong and could handle it. If it was like the movie, there would surely be others there who recognized me. That would be my ticket to easy street because everyone wants to suck up to a celebrity. I could even bribe one of the guards to leak my whereabouts. The judge didn't think of that part.

"Although I was instructed not to take personal items, I packed a suitcase with several outfits and a bunch of makeup. I put in my mp3 player, laptop and cell phone, the basics for my survival. If nothing else, I wanted to be prepared in case they let me use my own clothes. The judge thought I would be in a prison uniform but I was sure I would be treated differently than others at the camp. I felt good about my upcoming adventure and got a good night's sleep."

"I lived with Jeremy in his house. He has a two-bedroom home with a bedroom at each end of the house. I have my own bathroom and pretty much live like I'm on my own. He let me come and go as I please as long as I made all the appointments he set up for me. Since I'm home schooled in my real life, a tutor comes to the house several days a week. I don't have enough time to go to school with both shows going. I probably would have ended up in foster care after my grandmother got sick without Jeremy becoming my guardian. Life really was pretty good. What else could a teenager want?"

I couldn't help but notice a hint of sadness in her eyes before she shook it off and continued. This girl has already experienced a lot in her young life.

"At 5:00 A.M. the doorbell rang, waking me from a sound sleep. The police were at the door waiting to take me away. Judge Mark said within twenty-four hours, but hadn't specified a particular time. That was the first moment I felt he might have played us. Having the police show up at 5:00 A.M. assured no TV cameras or reporters to capture the event. Yesterday's court appearance had been covered already and there was no new news. No one stood on the lawn to get the shot of me being placed in handcuffs and put in the squad car. That would have been a money shot. I got in with no fanfare and off I went.

"After a three-hour car ride, we arrived at a police station, but I didn't know where. An officer processed me into the system, and I had to change into an orange jump suit, making me look like any other common inmate. My jewelry, cell phone and all electronics were inventoried and placed in a bag, which I had to sign. The bag and the rest of my clothes went into a storage locker. I didn't expect any of them to be returned."

I wasn't sure if she didn't trust the police or maybe she didn't trust anyone at this point. "Why didn't you expect those items to be returned? The police had them locked up, didn't they?"

"I had fans who would pay a pretty price for those personal items and it wouldn't have been surprising to learn they were stolen from the locker."

"Sorry for the interruption. Please continue."

She nodded slightly and went on. "I was taken to another car and introduced to two more officers who drove me to the work camp, which was another four-hour ride. We got breakfast from a McDonalds and we were on our way. At that point I realized Jeremy and my lawyer didn't know where I was. The two guards in the front wouldn't talk to me unless I asked a question and then only responded with short answers. I figured they were rent-a-cops doing a job so I stopped wasting my time trying to get them to talk. The drive took forever. I looked out the window, but I got bored fast. They didn't even play the radio.

"I saw where we crossed into Pennsylvania. The area was flat with not much to see. Finally, we stopped at a mall and one of the officers took out a cell phone and punched in a number then handed the phone back to me. Judge Mark was on the other end. He repeated the terms of my work detail, explaining it was not an ordinary camp and I was expected to contribute like everyone else. No special treatment would be given. He went over the fact that I was not to talk to anyone I came in contact with about who I was except those I work with or for. I laughed as he talked. He evidently didn't know anything about star power. People will bend over backwards just to talk to you. He had no idea how popular I really am.

"Judge Mark also went over the fact that Jeremy had signed over legal custody to him for four months. If I got into any trouble, he would be my guardian, but I would have no contact with him for at least four months. He reminded me if I stayed out of trouble during those four months and was ready, I could get out on good behavior. He also described the place where I would be housed as minimum security and that if I ran away all deals were off. His last statement was that life as I knew it was over. He wished me well and said, 'Goodbye, Alex.'"

Alexandria looked at me and said, "I had a feeling that something was wrong. Have you ever felt like you were being played, but you can't figure out how it's being done? Like the bottom is about to drop out but you think you are fine?"

I laughed. "Funny you should ask, because I had that same feeling not long ago."

She continued her story. "I knew we were in a rural area, a small town of some sort. We headed out of town. About twenty minutes later we arrived at my so-called work camp. It was a farm. Not like a work camp or prison farm, but a real farm. There were animals in pens standing right in the front yard. We pulled up next to a farm house with an odd appearance, but I couldn't put my finger on it. There was no one outside.

"One of the officers turned and said we had reached our destination. He reminded me what Judge Mark said about running away and going to jail for three years with no chance of an early release. In my best sarcasm, I told him I understood. He opened the door, let me out, then drove away. That's when the bottom fell out."

Seeing her fidget with the frayed trim on the upholstered chair, I felt we needed to take a break. "Let's stop for a couple of minutes. I need a cup of coffee. Do you want anything? Maybe a water?"

"Okay. A water would be nice. Thank you."

SEVEN

With coffee and water in hand, I returned to my office to find Alexandria with hands clasped and her eyes focused on the floor as if in prayer. I almost hated to disturb her, but I needed to hear the rest of her story. "Uh...Alexandria...are you okay to continue?"

She accepted the water, opened the bottle and took a quick sip. "Yes sir. I'm ready when you are."

"Good, let's move on then. Did you know where you were?"

"Not immediately. I stood in the driveway alone before grasping the reality of what was happening. That's when the door opened and Jonathon, my keeper, came out of his house. He was a large man who walked with confidence towards me. His size didn't scare me but his clothing did. The blue shirt and black pants and a set of black suspenders that all looked homemade. Black boots, straw hat, and a long beard confirmed my fears. I had read about these people but somehow thought they were fictional characters in a story. I was on a real Amish farm."

"Seriously, you weren't familiar with the Amish? Rural Pennsylvania is home to many communities." I added a bit of bravado since I didn't want to appear inept. Truth is, there's still a lot I don't understand.

"No. Just the little bit I read in school," she said. "My mind raced as I tried to remember what I had read about them. No electricity came to mind quickly. I glanced at the house and realized there were no overhead wires going to the house. Could they really live without electricity? Televisions, cell phones and video games all need electricity. Isn't water heated by electricity? What about the refrigerator and light bulbs? You have got to have electricity. How could you survive without it? The electricity at home had gone out for an hour or so a couple of times in the past and it was terrible.

"The yard was beat up without much green grass. There were fences all over the place. The only open area was the driveway. A big barn looked run down at first. Then I noticed the building was in good repair but was surrounded by a bunch of old equipment. It looked and felt dirty, or maybe it was the smell. I could feel the bottom dropping out.

"Animals inside the barn made a lot of noise. A mother chicken came out followed by about ten baby chickens. I remembered the mother was called a hen and babies were chicks. Other than dogs and cats, I had never been around animals except at the zoo. They looked cute as they scurried around their mother. She kept pecking at the ground, then stopping in one place and raking her feet across the ground searching for food. The chicks ran around her but did not go more than about eighteen inches from her. She had a moving circle around her. They were not leaving her protection.

"Jonathon noticed me watching the hen and he walked quickly towards her. Somehow, she called her chicks, they immediately ran under her wings and she sat down and covered them all. She was protecting them from him. He went close to her and slowly raised his boot as if to kick her. All of the sudden she jumped off her chicks and lunged at him. She grabbed his boot with her claws and held on. She beat his leg by flapping her wings and made loud sounds. She also pecked at his boot with her beak. She was taking on the large man with all she had. He jumped back a step and the hen released her grip and ran back to her chicks. She made the man retreat. She called her chicks and they all scurried away.

"He saw my shock at what he had just done. He said, 'My name is Mr. Yoder to you. I wanted you to see how protective that mother hen would be if I threatened her chicks. Even though I could have crushed her with one stomp she was willing to give up her life to save her offspring. My family and community are everything to me. I will do anything to protect them. You are only here because of a favor I owe to Mark. I understand, Alex, that you have no morals and do not understand right from wrong.

You are here to work for us. No one here cares who you are. You are a spoiled nobody to us. We do not want you here. This is not a vacation. If you decide not to work, you will not eat. I decide the rules for you. Rule number one is never mess with my family. Do you understand?'"

Simply hearing Alexandria's story made the hairs on the back of my neck stand up. *She must've been scared to death at that moment,* I thought. "What did you do?"

"You know that part about the bottom falling out? There was nothing beneath my feet. I was tumbling into an unknown abyss. I wasn't in Kansas anymore and I sure wasn't Dorothy. No wizard was going to save me. The reality of what Judge Mark had set up hit me like a punch to the stomach. No one knew where I was. I could not run away. He had played Jeremy, my lawyer and me. I was screwed. All I could do was nod my head to signify my understanding. 'Supper is a few hours away. My wife is inside waiting for you,' was all he said. Then he just walked off towards the barn."

"What kind of an introduction was that? That must have been hard to take," I said.

"Yes, it was. He let me know right away that I was not welcome. I didn't know what else to do so I started towards the house. Two little girls came out and stopped suddenly when they saw me. One appeared to be about seven or eight and the other maybe four years old. Both wore long dresses that went almost to the ground. They had little bonnets covering their hair. They also looked like they were wearing small boots. It was summer. Why were they wearing boots? Immediately, both of them looked at the ground and the older one took the lead and they walked past me without making eye contact. I felt like a leper.

"I entered the house through what must be a living room. Chairs sat around the edge of the wood floor. A candle sat on a table between the chairs. A throw rug in the center of the room and a couple of old paintings on the walls were the only decoration. The room was pretty sparse. Everything was in its place. I heard someone moving around in the kitchen. I turned left and headed that way.

"Inside the kitchen a woman watched some pots on the gas stove. The heat in the room was stifling. There was no fan to move the air. She also wore a long dress a few inches from the ground. She did not wear a bonnet but had her hair pulled back in a bun with a cloth covering pinned over it. When she noticed me, she pointed to the back room. I went to the doorway and saw a small metal tub with water in it. It was barely big enough to get in, but I quickly understood it was bath time for me. She poured in some hot water and slid a partition between the tub and the doorway.

"I went in the room and she closed the door. I took off my orange jumpsuit, laid it on the chair and went behind the screen and got in the tub. There was a bar of soap, wash cloth and towel on a little table beside the tub. It felt good to relax in a hot tub after the long morning. I soaked awhile and thought about my surroundings. It could be worse. At least I get to bathe alone instead of the group showers at the other place. After a good scrubbing, I was finished. I toweled off and went around the partition and noticed my orange jumpsuit was gone. I had not heard anyone open the door or come in. In its place was a long light blue dress, a pair of black socks and black boots. My panties were gone and a pair of white granny panties lay under the dress. I held up the dress and saw it was close to my size. Since there was nothing else to wear, I put it on. At that point I felt they would treat me as one of the family, but I still wasn't sure what that meant.

"They probably expected a fight from me over the clothing but the only other thing I had to wear was the jumpsuit, so why would I fight for that? There was a pile of hair pins and rubber bands so I tied my hair back in a pony tail. If they thought I was going to fight about that, they were also wrong. I could outsmart these hicks. I put on my socks and boots and opened the door into the kitchen."

I flipped the page on my legal pad. "Was that your plan, to outsmart people who didn't measure up to your standards? Was that the Alex persona coming through?" I asked. "It certainly doesn't match the girl sitting here today, but we can discuss that later. So, you went back into the kitchen?"

"Yes, I did. The woman still didn't speak but pointed at two laundry baskets sitting by the back door. A teenage girl dressed like me was helping her mother. She appeared to be about fifteen years old. The girl motioned for me to follow her. At the back door she stopped and handed me a bonnet like I saw the two younger girls wearing. I watched how she put hers on top of her head and tied it then she waited for me to do the same before going outside. I decided it was easier to conform then to start a fight. I would pick my battles from those I thought I could win. This one seemed to be nonnegotiable so I put the bonnet on.

"Outside were four long clothes lines filled with laundry. All the clothing was made out of the same blue or black fabric. I examined the shirts and pants and knew they were hand sewn. The hook closures on the shirts were not perfectly aligned. The pants didn't have zippers but had buttons on the front instead.

"I had never folded much laundry but it wasn't rocket-science. The girl began the task immediately and turned towards me so I could see how the items should be folded. I took down a shirt and folded it as she had. She nodded her head to confirm it was acceptable. I put it in my basket. The girl was much faster and filled her basket when mine was only half full. She rotated her finger in the air, which meant I was to keep going while she went inside the house with her basket. I continued folding and in about two minutes she returned with an empty basket. I only needed two more things and my basket would be full. She dropped in the last shirt to top off my basket and picked it up. Because her hands were full, she gave me the circular motion with her head, instructing me to keep folding. I got the idea we were in a rhythm. Each time she returned, she helped finish my basket carrying it inside and leaving me with the empty one to fill.

"When she returned the second time, I told her my name was Alex but she ignored me. She actually turned away and lowered her head to avoid eye contact. I knew she heard me because I was only two feet away so I figured she wasn't allowed to talk to me. So much for being part of the family."

Curiosity got the best of me. "Did any of the family members speak to each other?"

"No one spoke in my presence."

I nodded my acknowledgement and she continued.

"There were eight baskets of laundry by the time everything was taken from the lines and folded. The clothes ranged in size from men's pants and shirts and women's dresses to boy's pants and shirts and little girl's dresses. There were also cloth diapers, meaning there was a baby in the house.

"The bonnets came off at the door and hung on a nail just inside the doorway. I followed her upstairs to a bedroom. I saw two small beds in the room, one on one side and one on the other side with a small walkway between them. There was a closet and a dresser in the room. We had folded the girl clothes last so I figured these were hers. She hung up the dresses, some large and some small, and put the rest of the things in the dresser. This meant she shared the room with one of the smaller girls. As soon as we were done, we took the baskets downstairs and placed them in the room I had bathed in.

"The woman sat at the table peeling potatoes, so when the girl sat down and started peeling, I took my cue from her and sat down too. A paring knife was handed to me and the woman got up and put pots and pans on the stove. I knew she was beginning the evening meal.

"We peeled and diced ten potatoes, all in complete silence. The woman added them to a pot of water on the stove. The girl brought over a handful of washed carrots from the sink and we peeled those also. I could tell by the odd sizes that they were homegrown. Usually, the ones in the store are all the same size and length. These were not. Some were short and fat and some were long and skinny. When we were done, the girl got up and headed for the back door again. She looked my way and I followed. We stopped at the door to put on our bonnets.

"We walked outside where the girl started clapping her hands, which brought the yard alive. Chickens and ducks came running, clucking and quacking loud enough to wake the dead. The two little girls fell in line behind us and we all headed into the barn. Poultry of all sizes congregated in swarms outside the barn door while the noise grew in intensity. We entered a room with large piles of grain. The older girl grabbed a five-gallon bucket and scooped up grain and handed it to me. It was very heavy. Then she grabbed another five-gallon bucket and scooped up some for her to carry. The little girls each grabbed smaller buckets and filled them from the next grain bin. I could tell they were scooping corn into their buckets.

"We all filed out of the barn and the younger girls stopped at the crowd of ducks and chickens, which had worked themselves into a frenzy at this point. The girls tossed kernels of corn out into the crowd. All the chickens ran to where the corn was thrown and greedily ate it up. I followed the older girl and we went around to the back side of the barn to a long wooden trough for feeding large animals. She dumped her bucket in and looked at me. I did the same and we walked back to the barn.

"When we got back to the grain bin, she held up three fingers, signaling we needed three more trips to fill the trough. She filled both of our buckets then motioned to me then to the other buckets. I thought she was kidding at first by wanting me to carry two buckets at the same time. My eyes widened at the thought. When she realized my doubt at carrying two buckets, she grabbed both buckets and headed quickly for the door. She stopped, set them down and looked at me. Since she was smaller than me, I wasn't about to be out done and picked up both buckets and headed around the barn. They were heavy but I managed. When I got to the back, I realized she had not followed me. I thought I would be stuck doing all the hard work while she helped the little girls with the chickens. That wasn't going to happen."

EIGHT

Alexandria's descriptions of events that happened months ago, helped me understand what she had been through. Although these were now in her past, there were moments I could still detect exasperation in her voice. At this point, all I could offer was an empathic ear as she continued.

"I dumped the feed in the trough and headed back inside, but the girl was nowhere to be seen. Refilling my buckets, I returned back outside with plans to tell her a thing or two as soon as I saw her. No one was going to make me their slave.

"When I reached the outside, I was amazed to find her carrying two more five-gallon buckets, not filled with grain but water. Her expression showed the strain of carrying them. She stopped by the barn door and poured some of the water into a pan. The pan was about four-inches high and about two-feet across. Chickens and ducks swarmed to get a drink. I had never seen animals acting like this. To drink they all put their faces into the water then tipped their heads high and back to make the water flow down their throats. A few jumped into the pan as if it was the first water they had ever drank. They pushed and shoved as they mobbed the pan to drink. Each chicken and duck was out for themself.

"She poured water from the full bucket to the now half-empty bucket to level them out and headed towards the back of the barn. I followed, stopping at the trough to dump my grain buckets while she went another ten feet and poured her water into a large tank. She wiped her forehead with her sleeve and headed back. Needing four more buckets of grain, I headed for my part of the barn. Carrying grain wasn't so bad. I filled two buckets and deposited the grain into the trough with the rest.

"Crossing paths again, I held up one finger to indicate I needed one more trip to complete the grain quota. It was all she could do to carry two five-gallon buckets of water. I wanted to help but had my own job to finish.

"I poured my third and final batch of grain into the trough and was going back to find the girl when I heard a horse whinny. I stopped in my tracks as six harnessed horses came around the corner of the barn, walked past me and headed around to the back side. These were not like the horses pulling carriages through the park. These horses were huge and looked like they could walk right over me. They had a long stride and stepped in unison. Over the other barn noises, I heard a small voice yell, 'HO.' The horses all took one more step and stopped. Wet from sweat, they hung their heads and blew out deep breaths. It was difficult to believe, but a boy of about twelve or thirteen years old was driving them. He was smaller than me. They would crush him like a bug if they stepped on him.

"About that time, the girl came around with two more buckets of water and as soon as the horses saw her, they bobbed their heads up and down and started pawing at the ground. The boy once again yelled 'HO' and they settled down. They obviously wanted some of the water she was carrying. She emptied her buckets into the tank and headed for more.

"The little girls came around back and stood behind the horses. I was afraid for them but no one else seemed to give it a thought. The older girl glanced at me and I followed. We went around the barn, past the remaining chickens and ducks still searching for any signs of a missed kernel of corn. A satisfying calm now resonated in both flocks.

"The older girl took my grain buckets, went inside the barn and came back out with two more five-gallon water buckets that matched hers. I knew at that point I would be hauling water, too and since I was bigger than her, I was sure I could handle it. She handed me the two new buckets, picked up hers and walked away. I followed behind her.

"We carried our buckets around the house to a rusty iron water pump. She placed the bucket under the spout and started moving the handle up and down. Water immediately poured out. Once the first bucket was full, she replaced it with the second. When both of hers were full, she placed my first bucket under the spout then stepped back and looked at me. It took me a second to understand that I was responsible for pumping water for my buckets. The long iron handle was cool to the touch. I pulled down. It resisted more than I expected but by putting my weight behind it I made it start pumping. Once started, it didn't take as much effort to keep it going. The water came flying out. I looked back at the girl and smiled. She got caught up in the moment and clapped her hands before realizing she had encouraged me and looked away. As the bucket filled, she moved her arm up and down as if pumping to let me know to keep going. She positioned my second bucket beside the first and just before over filling she yanked the full one out and slid the empty one in place. I didn't have to stop and restart the pump. I nodded my head, thanking her and once again she broke into a small smile.

"She then reached around the pole and took off a tin cup hanging on the side and put it under the water to fill it. She took a long drink and refilled it as I finished pumping. When I stopped, she handed me the full cup of water. I didn't want to drink after her but I was thirsty. I took the metal cup and tasted the water. It was amazingly cold. Almost to the point of freezing. It was so satisfying that I drank the whole thing. I glanced over to see her once again looking at me. When I finished, I handed the cup back and she hung it back on the pole. I nodded in appreciation and once again she smiled a little. We were starting to bond and I didn't even know her name.

"She grabbed her two full water buckets and headed towards the barn. I knew I was responsible for my two buckets. I grabbed both buckets and raised them off of the ground about an inch. They were all I could handle as I staggered forward. Remembering a gallon of water weighs about eight pounds, I quickly calculated we carried about forty-pounds in each hand. The girl was not even close to my size and yet she was moving twice as fast as me. I was determined not to let her out do me, so I mustered up my strength and walked forward.

"By the time I got to the edge of the barn I saw the two little girls carrying in parts of the harness used for driving the horses. It looked like all they could handle too. I rounded the back and saw the boy gathering all of the leather straps. He draped them around his neck and shoulders to carry them into the barn. There were a lot of straps, and I could tell he was straining with the load. This place was going to be a workout."

"You're not kidding," I said. "If I had a job like that, I wouldn't need a gym membership." Alexandria simply smiled at my lame attempt at humor.

She took a breath and continued. "My cohort rounded the back with empty buckets, and stopped to take mine. I tried to tell her I could handle them, but she grabbed the buckets and carried them to the water tank. She looked at me, signaling one more trip as she walked past with my empty buckets. I grabbed her empty ones and followed."

Alexandria held up her left hand. "My hands pulsed in agony from the bucket handle digging into my palms." Using her right index finger, she pointed to a faint red stripe across a hint of callous.

"At the well the girl put her bucket under the spout and started pumping. Without being told I readied her second bucket and when her first one was filled enough, I yanked it out and replaced it with the empty one. She nodded approval. As the next one approached the three-quarters mark she looked at me. Once again, I was confused. It should be my turn to pump. Finally, with no other alternative, she said, 'Switch the bucket.' The bucket was nearly full and I realized she wasn't going to stop pumping. I wasn't ready. As I scrambled to grab the third bucket, she saw my struggles but instead of slowing down she pumped faster.

"I saw a glint in her eye. She was challenging me. I grabbed the bucket and slammed the third one into place but not before water overflowed onto my boots. She laughed at what she saw. She continued pumping but slowed to a steady pace. As the third bucket approached the switching point, I was ready. The last transition went smoothly and as it reached the half full point she stopped. I looked up and she grabbed my first bucket and poured water into the half-full bucket until they were each three-quarters full. I shook my head thinking she was taking it easy on me. Ignoring my displeasure, she grabbed the full buckets and carried them off. I was not having it. I filled the one bucket with the other one and pumped the second one full as well.

"Having gotten past the adrenaline rush of our silent banter, I hoisted

54

the two full buckets and struggled back around the barn. By the time I got to the water tank, she had dumped her buckets. We had carried seventy gallons of water from the pump at the side of the house across the yard and around to the back of the barn.

"The young boy stood near the water tank and took my first bucket as I approached, dumping it in. He acted like it wasn't heavy at all. These people are strong. The tank was almost running over as he poured my second bucket. When it started to overflow, he stopped with half a bucket left. There was nothing else to do with it so he dumped it on the ground. My heart sank. My bullheadedness caused extra work for nothing. The other girl knew exactly how much we needed. She wasn't being nice to me, just practical. I felt my face heat up with anger but realized it was entirely my fault.

"The horses stood at the fence ready to be let into the pen so they could drink. We cleared the area as the boy opened the gate and the horses raced to the water. They jockeyed for spots and stood around the huge bowl side by side. Six thirsty horses drank heartily at the same time. My arms felt like they had been pulled out of their sockets from carrying the buckets. We all retreated into the barn and dropped off the buckets.

"Both sets of harness were hung so the chain links slipped over nails in the wall. The straight wooden pieces, which I learned later are called singletrees, were placed in the corner. All was well organized, ready for the next time.

"With the boy in the lead and me last, we headed towards the house. Bonnets came off as we entered the house. I could smell dinner cooking. My stomach growled at the prospect of eating. It smelled great. The boy went up the stairs and I followed the girl into the kitchen. She began removing dishes from the cupboard for the table. There was seating for twelve around the picnic-style table. The mother made a little clicking sound with her tongue and looked towards the corner. The girl responded by handing me a two-gallon bucket. She put her hand against the outside of the bucket marking the halfway point then made the pumping motion with her hand. I figured out that we needed half a bucket of water.

"I was almost to the well when the smallest girl ran up behind me and grabbed my dress from behind. When I turned, she stood there holding my bonnet. She thrust it into my hand. I had not thought about putting it on just to go to the well. Evidently, it was more important than I thought. I decided to try to break the ice with her. I told her thank you and asked her name. She didn't look away but shook her head back and forth. As I put on the bonnet, the small girl placed the bucket under the spout and tried to pump the water herself by hanging from the handle. She was trying so hard it made me giggle. She just didn't weigh enough. After securing my bonnet, I put my hand on the end of the handle and added the necessary effort.

"The girl quickly moved closer to the main pump and as it went down, she could stand and help me move the handle. Water came gushing out and we looked at each other and smiled. When the bucket was filled halfway we stopped. I gasped as the little girl tried to grab the bucket to carry it in. She used both hands and was grunting with all her might but was only able to move it a few inches. I smiled at her and asked if she could help me carry it. She looked up and smiled back as I grabbed the handle beside her hand and we both started to walk with it.

"As we headed towards the house, Mr. Yoder and another man entered the house. When we opened the back door, I took off the bonnet and hung it on the nail. The little girl nodded her approval as she let go of the bucket. Keeping her head down she started for the kitchen and I followed. In the kitchen the older girl took the bucket of water from me but didn't look at me. My almost new friends were dead silent.

"Part of the water went into a separate sink. The men went to the sink first and washed their hands. Then the women took their turn. We had worked hard, and the filth of the barn was all over us. I was last in line. The water was milky brown by the time I washed my hands. I wondered if I had removed dirt or added more.

"Mr. Yoder took his place at the head of the table. As everyone stood at their respective places I waited to see where I should sit. To my horror there were seven places set but eight of us. Mr. Yoder looked at me and said, 'Only family and invited guests sit at the table when we eat. You are neither. You will be eating in the back.'"

NINE

As Alexandria's attorney, I wasn't sure what to make of her description of her first meal with the Amish family. I knew the religious sect was strict, but this had me concerned. Withholding food was beyond a rational punsihment. "Calm my fears, Alexandria. Were you able to eat? What happened? Does Mark need to know about this?"

She gave no direct response to my questions, just a simple nod and slight smile before she continued. "At the time it felt like another punch in the stomach. Mr. Yoder pointed to the small room where I had bathed and I slowly turned and walked away. A small table was set up but there was no plate or silverware on it. The older girl went to the sink and poured the rest of the water from the bucket into glasses. The younger girls took the full glasses and deposited them at each place setting. The littlest girl brought me a glass of water without looking at me. They all sat down.

"I took the cue and sat at the little table in the back then waited and watched. Even though they were on both sides of the table they all joined hands, bowed their heads and prayed. I watched and listened as Mr. Yoder thanked his god for the food provided, the safety given to them and the family he had. When they finished the mother stood and brought bowls of food to the table.

"Mr. Yoder took a helping from each bowl and passed it down the line. It went from him to Mrs. Yoder then to a young man and his wife. From there to an older teenage boy then the boy who brought in the horses and then to each girl by age. The youngest girl got the last portion from each bowl. No one ate. They waited until everyone had their plate then he nodded and they all ate together.

"Mr. Yoder looked at his older daughter and softly asked how I did. She nodded her head yes and he nodded to his wife. I realized if she shook her head no, I would not be eating. None of them cared whether I ate or not. They had all worked hard and if I didn't pull my weight, I would go hungry.

"The mother got up and took another plate and set of silverware from the cupboard and put a portion from each bowl on it. She was scraping the bowls to get all that was left. There was not going to be any seconds. She then walked back to my room and sat it on my little table. She turned and went back to her seat and started her meal.

"My stomach growled as I looked down at the food. There was a small portion of sausage with some mashed potatoes, green beans and a biscuit. There was no butter or jam for the biscuit. No salt or pepper on the table. I wasn't going to ask for any. I dug into my meal like it was my last. I had not eaten since breakfast at McDonalds. I was famished and wolfed down the meal in a few minutes.

"When I was done, I saw Mr. Yoder watching me. I decided to win him over. With my biggest smile I looked right at him and gave him thumbs up to show I liked the meal. His expression never changed. He starred right at me. He did not blink. My thumbs went down and my smile went limp. I looked down at my plate. To him I was nothing. There were no equal rights in this house. I was only here because of Judge Mark. Mr. Yoder did not want me in his house or around his family. I sat quietly and waited.

"In about ten minutes they were finished. The men got up and went outside and the older girl picked up my plate. She gave the 'come with me' nod and I picked up the silverware and glass and walked behind her into the kitchen. She gave me the water bucket and pointed to almost the top. I realized I was heading back to the well again. As I headed for the door the little one, decided she would escort me. She jumped in front of me and led me to the back door. She held up her hand like a traffic cop and pointed towards the bonnets.

"She was my best candidate to win over. Seeing no one else around I grabbed her bonnet first. Her eyes widened. Before she could protest, I bent down and placed it on her head. I tied the front two parts together and patted her on the head. She accepted my mothering and smiled up at me. I took my bonnet and placed it on my head and we proceeded out to the well.

"Once again, she raced ahead of me and was hanging on the well handle trying to activate the pump. I placed the bucket under the spout and looked at her. She hung there looking at me. I smiled and told her to try harder. She pulled and jerked on the pump handle but didn't have enough weight to make it go down. She held on about two-thirds of the way towards the end of the handle so I grabbed her around the middle and moved her to the end of the handle. By increasing her leverage, her weight was enough to make the pump handle drop. Her eyes widened as she dropped to the ground. Quickly moving closer to the middle of the pump handle, she started the pump working. Once she had the necessary momentum, the effort was lessened and water spewed out into the bucket. I clapped as she worked the pump handle. She beamed back at me as she worked. I stepped up to help her but she shook her head, telling me she could fill the bucket.

"When she finished you could tell she was so proud. She tried to pick up the bucket of water but it was too heavy for her. I told her she did a good job and I would carry it in. She marched in front of me like I was carrying a great trophy that she had won.

"Inside, the older girl took the water, pouring half in one side of the sink and the other half in the other side. She brought over a pot of hot water from the stove adding that into the first sink. All of the dishes were piled on the counter. She handed me an apron and put one on herself. She washed while I rinsed and dried the dishes in silence. The little one wanted to tell her big sister what she had done but with me in the room no one was allowed to speak. The little girl eventually went outside.

"Looking around I saw that no one else was in the house, so I asked her name. She stopped and looked straight ahead. Then slowly she moved her head back and forth. She would not break her silence. She had spoken to me at the well so I knew she was capable."

What a lonely existence. As a lawyer I understood punishment was supposed to serve a purpose, but this was bordering on cruel and definitely unusual, at least from my point of view. "How long was this shunning supposed to last?"

"At the time, I had no idea. I just knew it would be a long four months if this continued. Here I was surrounded by a whole family, but I was still alone. Yet, the silence gave me a chance to reflect about my real life. I had thousands of fans and plenty of fake friends for the cameras but no real friends. Before becoming famous, I had a few friends at school but stopped talking to them a few years ago. How could I have so many people involved in my life and not one who really cares for me? Looking at it from that point, my life was pretty sad. Everything I did was planned for the internet. All my time was consumed by the shows. Filming two shows took all I had just to keep up. I was being pulled at both ends just to keep up."

"I bet a lot of people who wish for the type of fame you have never consider the other side, the lonely side," I said. "Perhaps, you can help someone avoid the same mistakes."

Her eyes glistened as a tear threatened to escape before her hand quickly brushed it away. "One day, I'm hoping to do just that, Mr. Woods."

Trying to maintain my own emotions, I had to look away. "Please go on. I believe you were washing dishes?"

"Yes sir. As we finished the dishes, the older girl motioned me to follow. She picked up another bucket in the corner that held all the potato and carrot peelings along with other things. I could tell it was garbage.

"We went back to the barn. As we approached, I heard pigs. There were two pens. The first one had two medium-size pigs milling around but they weren't dirty and nasty like I expected. Their white and black coats were free of mud or dirt and the pens were lined with clean straw. A feed trough at the front of the pen held some grain, but when the girl poured half the kitchen garbage on top, the pigs came right up and started eating it. She reached down and scratched the top of the first pig's head. It looked up, stopped eating and raised itself up on the trough so she could scratch the pig's neck and side. When the second pig saw what was happening it, too, wanted to be scratched and pushed as close as it could towards me. Not being accustomed to animals, I stepped back as the pig advanced to- ward me. The girl moved in between to appease both pigs at the same time.

The squeals could have wakened the dead. She made clucking noises at them. After about a minute she stepped back and they went back to eating.

"The second pen had a huge mother pig, called a sow, with a bunch of little babies. The girl dropped the rest of the slop into her trough. Since her piglets were nursing, she laid there for another thirty seconds then decided to get up. She was massive. She slowly made her way to the trough.

"The piglets ran around in the pen, moving too fast for me to count. The best I could do was eight or nine before the girl decided to help and held up ten fingers then two more. I asked if that meant twelve and she nodded. It was fun watching them scurry around and jump on each other. The bigger ones pushed the little ones around and the little ones squealed like they were being beat to death. I didn't have any brothers or sisters but figured human siblings acted similarly.

"After about a minute, the girl turned and walked away. I continued to watch the pigs and she stopped about six feet away and snapped her finger to get my attention. As we left the barn, she led me around to a side of the house I had not seen. I followed her and she turned and put her hand out to indicate a small red building standing off to itself. It was only about five-feet wide by five-feet long and eight-feet tall with a slanted tin roof.

"She opened the door wide. Inside was a low bench with a hole cut in the middle and a wooden toilet seat surrounding the hole. I suddenly realized it was an outhouse. I had never seen one before. The roof set a few inches above the top of the walls. A three-inch gap between allowed light to come in and air to circulate. I stood at the doorway looking in. She pointed at the seat but I shook my head no. She went in, lifted the lid and reached to the side where there was a bucket of white powder. She scooped up the white powder and sprinkled some inside the hole. Later, I learned the powder was lime. Knowing what was inside the hole, I realized she was showing me what to do when I needed that building. Everyone would eventually need that building. I glanced in and was relieved to see a couple of rolls of real toilet paper hanging on the wall. She went inside and closed the door as I waited outside.

"When she came out, we went over to the well. She opened a small wooden box attached below the tin cup and produced a bar of soap. She looked at me and I started pumping the water. Once she had soaped up and rinsed off, she handed the bar of soap to me and I did the same as she pumped the handle for me. It felt good to wash off. I had not even been there half a day but was glad it was almost over. The family had eaten and dishes were washed. The animals were watered and bedded down. It felt like a good time to unwind at the end of a long day."

Alexandria stopped talking for a moment. I laid my pen on top of the legal pad and looked at her. Her furrowed brow told of the exhaustion she felt that day. "Were you finally able to stop for the day and relax?"

She gazed at me as if to say, *Are you kidding?* With a brief shaking of her head, she continued. "We headed to a shed between the house and barn and she brought out a garden hoe for each of us. I knew at that point our day was not over. Beside the barn was a large garden. Since it was early May, seeds had sprouted and were breaking through the soil. I didn't know what the plants were, but you could tell what belonged and what did not. The girl showed me how to loosen the soil with the hoe and how to remove the weeds. This was a new experience and after a half hour I realized it was back-breaking work. Sweat ran down my body. Dirt rose up in little puffs each time my hoe dug into the soil, sticking to my clothes and creating a thin layer of muddy slime down my arms. You wouldn't think a tool weighing only a few pounds could become so heavy. Bending over and pulling the hoe into and across the dirt really works your arm muscles. Thank goodness the day was almost over.

"Near dusk the younger man came out of the barn and closed the doors that had been open all day long. The chickens and ducks had gone into the barn and all the animals were tucked in safely for the night. All was quiet. He headed into the house.

"We put our hoes in the shed before stopping at the outhouse. Once again we went to the well, washing our hands and attempting to remove the garden grime from our arms. Her not talking didn't prevent me from asking about taking another bath before going to bed. She stopped in front of me and turned around. I understood her one-finger gesture to mean only one bath a day. For a second, she stared at me in disbelief and then she smiled and shook her head back and forth. She again held up one finger. Confused, I looked at her, then it dawned on me. 'Once a week?' I blurted out. She smiled and nodded as she turned for the house. I was going to be pretty rank in a week.

"I followed her upstairs where she changed into a long nightgown-type garment. She handed one to me. It resembled a large cloth bag with arm holes and a place to stick your head through. Our dresses from that day were hung in the closet next to the clean ones, telling me they would be worn again. This was going to take some getting used to. Since it was almost dark, she pointed towards the bed on the opposite side of the room where I would sleep. Not seeing a clock in the room, and with it not being fully dark yet, I asked about the time. She just shrugged her shoulders and climbed into her own bed. Apparently, all we needed to know was that it was bedtime. Since I was really tired, I didn't think I would have any problem falling asleep.

"I remembered small dresses hanging in the closet so this bed must have been for one of the smaller girls. Just about then the two little girls came into the room wearing similar sleeping garments. The older of the two climbed in bed with the teenage girl and the youngest girl pulled my blankets back and wiggled her way in with me. The bed was not nearly big enough for two people. I lay scrunched against the wall while she got comfortable. To be such a little girl, her body radiated a lot of heat. I threw off the cover and lay there exhausted but unable to sleep. Eventually, I fell asleep even though my bed partner kept tossing and turning.

"Finally, sound asleep, I dreamed someone was pushing and hitting me so hard that I woke up. The little girl was hitting me. When she realized I was awake she pulled at my arm, trying to roll me out of bed. After I got my bearings, I asked what she wanted, but she kept pulling on my arm. I asked, 'What?' No answer just more pulling. I finally asked loudly, 'What do you want?' In a small weak voice I heard, 'I need to go to the outhouse.' Without opening my eyes, I rolled over. 'Then go,' I told her. She started sobbing and I heard her whisper, 'I'm afraid.' I instantly felt about two inches tall. Of course, she was too small to go outside in the dark by herself. I apologized.

"As I got out of bed, it felt like my whole body was on fire. She took my hand, and we slowly went downstairs. My muscles screamed with every step. I didn't know what time it was other than nighttime. It was dark so the time really didn't matter. A full moon provided enough light to find our way.

"We put on our boots and went to the outhouse. She left the door open a little to make sure I didn't leave her. After she was done, I asked her if she wanted a drink of water and she said, 'Yes, please.' Without thinking, she actually answered my question verbally instead of shaking her head. It was so nice to be spoken to even if it was from a little girl. I quietly asked, 'What is your name, sweetie?' She replied in a small voice, 'Hanna.' I said, 'Well, Hanna, let's get us a drink.' We went to the well and we pumped out a cup of that cool water. She drank first and I finished it up. It was very refreshing.

"She took my hand again as we went inside. I was flying high going back upstairs with my new friend. We snuggled into bed next to each other. I put my arm around her and she nestled into my side. I never had brothers or sisters. The closeness was overwhelming. I laid there listening to and feeling her breath in and out. After a few minutes, her breathing became slow and regular. She was a sleep. I knew she had crossed a line and I would keep the knowledge of her name to myself. I finally dozed off."

TEN

"I woke to the sound of girls skittering around in the room getting dressed. It was not quite light outside, but the sun was peeking over the horizon. I almost asked what time it was, but remembered there was not a clock anywhere that I had seen. I tried to stretch my arms but my muscles had stiffened during the night. My whole body felt as if it had been beaten with a baseball bat. I wasn't in as good of shape as I thought.

"I got up and put on my dress from the day before. Following the example set before me, I started to make the bed as the seven-year-old made her bed. When I began arranging the blankets, Hanna grabbed me by the hand and shook her head. I looked at the older girl and she also shook her head. The older girl motioned for me to follow her out of the bedroom. As we left, I saw Hanna climb on top of the bed and arrange the covers. Evidently, bedmaking was a job for the little girls. I knew at that point if they had their jobs, we had ours.

"I followed the older girl downstairs to the back door. Bonnets went on and we headed to the outhouse, then to the well to wash up and for a quick drink. The sun was just beginning to rise over the horizon. Except for hurting all over and stinking from yesterday's sweat, it felt nice to be up. I had never been up to see the sunrise. What an amazing time of day."

These early morning meetings with Alexandria, gave me a new appreciation for sleeping late. "You are so right," I said, while trying hard not to yawn. "I've experienced the sunrise myself, the last couple of weeks."

A flicker of confusion crossed her face before she continued. I don't think she understood my sarcasm.

Alexandria continued her story. "We headed toward the barn. The animals were awake and moving around. The horses lined up in their stalls, poking their heads through to a trough. We climbed a wooden ladder to a loft and pitched hay down to the barn floor. We each had a pitch fork and dust flew everywhere. My muscles were screaming, but I tried to keep up. Finally, the girl stopped and threw her pitch fork down like a javelin on top of the pile and it stuck straight up. A perfect shot. She glanced at me and I threw mine down. It hit at the right angle but didn't have enough force to stand and slowly slumped to one side then toppled over. She rocked one hand back and forth, giving me the so-so gesture. Although she was younger, she challenged me to best her.

"We went down the ladder and forked hay into the troughs for the horses. The older boy slid another door open revealing two cows. They had their own pen and their heads poked through waiting for hay. He sat down on a small stool and started milking the first cow. The girl headed that way with some hay so I followed with more. I had never seen anyone actually milk a cow. He made it look easy as milk squirted into the metal bucket, making a pinging sound when it hit. He saw I was watching but didn't acknowledge my presence. We deposited our hay and went back to the horses.

"The little girls showed up, got their buckets and started feeding the chickens and ducks. Once again there was a flurry of wings and noises like they had not been fed in a week. We grabbed the water buckets and went out to the well. I pumped and the girl moved the buckets until we had four five-gallon buckets full. While the last bucket filled, she took the tin cup off the nail, filled it up and drank the water. She placed the cup back on the nail as the bucket was approaching the three-fourth mark. Then she looked at me and raised her eyebrows. I made my eyes bulge as big as I could then remembered I could speak. This code of silence didn't pertain to me. I looked right at her and said, 'I know you're going to fill that cup up for me.' She broke into a smile and grabbed the cup just as the bucket was full. The last pump filled the cup. I took a long pull on the water cup and then with one big gulp, emptied it. I knew at that point we would become friends. I like someone with a little spunk.

"We hauled the water into the barn, stopping to fill the chicken and ducks' water bowl and the rest went into the cows' water trough. The boy had switched to the second cow and now had almost half a bucket of milk. We went back to the horses and finished distributing the hay we had thrown down.

"The girl made a half mark on her bucket for water and looked at me expectantly. I gave her my best *I don't have a clue what you want* look and she moved her hand back and forth like she was sawing the bucket in half. I shrugged my shoulders like I still had no clue. She sawed again. I asked, 'Do you need a saw?' She made a motion like she was drinking from a cup. Finally, I smiled and said, 'Oh, you need another half bucket of water. Why didn't you say so?' Then she realized I was messing with her. She gave me the *Okay, you got me* head nod.

"She was at the front of the barn carrying two buckets of a grain mixture. She split my water between the buckets and stirred the contents with a big stick, turning it into a thick, sloppy slurry. She picked up the two buckets and headed for the last part of the barn where two pens held three pigs in one space and one huge pig in another. She split the slop between the two pens. Once again, the animals acted like they had not eaten for a week. She pointed to yet another water tank sitting between the two pens. I headed out of the barn, grabbed my two buckets and went for water. The sun was completely up. It was early May but morning temperatures were still low and the air had a crisp feel. The breeze made it just a little nippy outside.

"The girl was over with the horses opening the back door and letting them out into the pasture. Two of the younger horses actually romped around as they welcomed the new day. The horses had come in last night completely tired but a good night's sleep and some feed had rejuvenated them, and they were ready to go. I rubbed my soar arms and thought about the old saying, *What does not kill you will make you stronger.* It is supposed to inspire you to get through the tough times, but they fail to point out that some may die! Hopefully, I will be one that makes it through.

"With all the animals tended to, we veered towards the well to wash our hands before going into the house. Hanna had a three-gallon water bucket under the faucet and she was hanging on the end of the pump handle to get it started. She wiggled a little and it activated. As the handle came down, she quickly jumped off and positioned herself closer to the middle and started pumping the water. The older girl looked at her in amazement and Hanna beamed back at her and me. I told her how good she was doing and how much help she was. I grabbed the bucket and started walking with it. Hanna grabbed the side of the handle and helped me carry it. She was very proud of what she had done.

"Coming in from the cool morning air, the house felt warm and comforting. I smelled breakfast and followed the girl into the kitchen to see scrambled eggs cooking, bacon frying and warm bread sitting on the stove. There were no plates out, so I went to the cabinet and opened it. I looked at the girl. She nodded her head and held up nine fingers. I counted out nine plates and nine cups for water. I went around the table and set out the nine place settings. I placed the silverware and filled the cups with water.

"The girl set the food, butter and homemade jam on the table. The two little girls quickly went to bring everyone inside. When everyone showed up, I counted nine people plus me. The family consisted of Jonathon and his wife, the three girls, two boys and a young man and woman who were evidently married. My heart dropped as I realized there were only nine plates set out at the main table. The mother took one more plate from the cupboard and started to put food on it.

"She put scrambled eggs, bacon and two pieces of bread on my plate. She handed me a fork and a water glass then stood by her chair. When Jonathon sat down, everyone followed his example. They all bowed their heads and he said a prayer. When he finished, they all started passing the food bowls around to fill their plates.

"I went to the sink and filled my water glass from the bucket and went into the corner room and sat down and ate. Since I was hungry the food tasted great but the lump in my throat prohibited my eating. I felt like crying. This family would not even let me sit at the same table as them. I decided to work hard, keep my head down and do my time. I swallowed hard and pushed the food down my throat."

ELEVEN

From my perspective Alexandria had fallen into a difficult routine with little to no interaction with the family and not much more in the way of nourishment. "Did anything change? It appears Hanna was warming up to you, but what about the others? Were they at least beginning to accept your presence?" I was almost afraid to ask those questions, but did so nevertheless.

"The next three days were pretty much the same. Get up early, feed and water the animals, do more chores, cooking, cleaning and the never-ending work in the garden. Then go to bed at dark and get up at dawn the next day to start all over. Jonathon and the younger boy went to the fields all day. The young man and the older boy left the farm, walked down the road after breakfast and returned just before dusk. Since no one talked to me I had no idea how they spent the day. My only comfort was with Hanna. She walked with me when doing choirs and held my hand sometimes. My heart warmed every time she came around. She was my only friend.

"On the fourth day, Hanna came and got me out of the garden around mid-morning. We went into the house. She pointed at a basket and a water jug waiting for us. I picked them up and followed her out of the house. We walked down the drive and to the road. I knew from the previous three days that someone delivered lunches to Jonathon and the son working in the fields. Even though it was about a mile walk, it felt good to get out of the garden for a while.

"As we approached the first field the boy's horses were standing still by some trees. As we moved closer, we saw him bending down, trying to free a large tree limb lodged in the equipment. He yelled at the horses and they started to move. The farm implement began to move but the limb became bound up. The horses put their backs into it and pulled harder, snapping the limb in half. The limb shot out from under the rig with great force. Half of it hit the boy in the leg just below the knee. He went down.

"Horrified, we ran to him. He had passed out. I saw the bone sticking out below his knee and looked around for Jonathon but couldn't see him. I asked Hanna if she knew where he was. She pointed in a direction of a hill. I asked if she could go get him, she nodded and ran toward the hill."

Although my only knowledge of the accident was through Alexandria's interpretation, I had to look away. It wasn't something I readily admitted, especially to a client, but that type of thing made me queasy, especially when a child was involved. "You must have been scared to death. Was there anything you could do to help the boy?"

"As Alexandria we made a lot of videos for people to watch online. If we made it, they would pay to watch it. Remember, I told you there was a series on first aid, which went over so well we added more episodes covering everything from basic stuff to more advanced training. I knew what to do. I laid him on his back and elevated his head and checked the injury. I grabbed two branches from the nearby tree and lined up his leg as close as I could. I set the sticks opposite of each other and used my hair bonnet ties to fasten them in place. It was not pretty but the leg was splinted.

"He started to come around. I told him to not move and everything would be alright. He passed out again. When he awoke the next time, he screamed in pain. I took off my bonnet, wet it and dabbed his forehead. He cried with the pain. I tried to tell him he would be alright, but his eyes turned on me in anger. He yelled for me not to touch him. I knew he was in great pain and let him vent at me. He passed out again.

"Jonathon crested the hill running toward us and called to his son. He was moving fast. Approaching, he only saw me hovering over the boy. His emotions and adrenaline were really pumping. He yelled for me to stay away and wanted to know where my head covering was. I backed up. Seeing his son lying there unconscious, Jonathon's eyes were wild with anger and desperation. He exploded at me. 'What have you done?'

"I understood he didn't know the whole story. I explained the boy had been in an accident just as we arrived and that he was unconscious from the broken leg which I had splinted. I tried to reassure him the boy would be alright, but we needed to stay calm and call EMS to come and get him. Jonathon just stood there frozen. He didn't know what to do.

"I felt Hanna grab my hand and realized this would likely be traumatic for her. My training kicked in. I told Jonathon we must call for help and his son needs a doctor. Jonathon came out of his haze, looked at me and said, 'We have to take him to the doctor ourselves.' Taking charge, he bent over his son and started to lift him.

"Instinctively I placed my hands on his back and pushed down keeping him from picking up his son. I yelled, 'NO.' He stepped back and screamed, 'What you are doing.' I looked him right in the eye and calmly said, 'He has a compound fracture. The bone is sticking out of the skin. This type of injury can be hard to heal. We must be careful not to move the leg or it will cause more damage and may not heal properly.' He was stunned by both my answer and the way I had taken charge, but realized I knew more about the situation than him. Grasping that in his culture a woman never speaks to a man like that, I looked down at the ground and said in a subservient voice, 'We must move him correctly. Please let me help you.'

"His shoulders dropped and his demeanor changed. He took a couple of deep breaths and said, 'Okay, what do we need to do?' I explained that when he picked up the boy, I would hold up the leg to keep it from moving.

"We walked slowly side by side. We did not talk. The boy woke up and saw his father. He whimpered from the pain. As we approached the farm house, he told Hanna to go get her mother. She ran ahead. By the time we hit the driveway her mother and sister met us at the end of the fences. He told the older girl to get the buggy ready. She quickly realized the situation and ran to the barn without questions. We carried him to the buggy and placed him in the back seat. The girl brought out a horse and began hitching it up. I was still holding up the leg. I looked at the mother and explained it needed to be kept as still as possible. She got up in the back seat and slid herself under his legs so they rested on her lap. I told her not to let him move the broken leg, she must keep it still. She nodded and placed her hands firmly on his splint. Jonathon got in the driver's seat and off they went.

"I looked over and the girl was looking at me. I asked her about bringing the horses from the fields. She nodded and pointed towards the well. While she went into the house, Hanna and I got ourselves a cold drink.

"When she returned, she had another head bonnet for me. It actually felt good to have one back on my head. It provided shade and kept my head cool. She looked at Hanna and asked if she wanted to stay with Ruth. I realized the married younger woman with the baby was still in the house. I figured that was her name. Hanna stepped next to me and grabbed my hand. The girl went to her other side and grabbed Hanna's other hand and said, 'Okay.' We headed to the field hand in hand in hand.

"The boy's horses stood right where we left them. So, we headed over the hill in the direction where I had sent Hanna to find Jonathon. I expected to see the horses standing in the next field but when we crested the hill my heart sank. Jonathon's horses were almost a quarter mile away. The thought of little Hanna running by herself all that way made me sick. For a little girl she had done an amazing feat. I know these people are tough, but she was so little. She took off by herself as soon as I had asked her to."

"How old is she?" I asked.

"Four."

I shook my head in disbelief. "Oh my! She's not only tough but brave to run that far by herself. The kids that age in my neighborhood barely go outside." I nodded for her to continue.

"The girl walked around the team of horses to check them out. I told her the accident was with the first horses. She pulled back a long lever to raise the disks from the soil. She positioned herself behind the horses with the reins in hand and yelled 'Get up.' The horses started walking and as they did the equipment rose out of the ground on its wheels. We went to the end of the field and she yelled 'Whoa.' The horses stopped and she unhitched the equipment.

"She drove the horses back to the first field, stopping at the site of her brother's accident and his team of horses. We had not spoken about what happened and I knew she had questions so I picked up the two large sticks and explained how they were lodged in the farm implement and how the broken limb flew into his leg. I pointed to where Hanna and I were when we saw it all happen. I told her about his broken leg and that he should be okay She looked at the horses, the equipment, and the pieces of wood, reconstructing the situation in her mind. I could tell she put it together. She looked at me and actually said, 'So there is nothing wrong with the disk?' Hearing her speak surprised me. I told her I didn't think there was. She had the horses move the disk about twenty feet. After making sure it operated correctly, she engaged the lever, and the disk came up out of the ground and she stopped the horses. She unhooked the equipment from the horses and drove them over to the shade with the other horses.

"Since we were out in the field with only Hanna to hear, I took a chance and asked her name. She looked at the ground trying to decide whether to break the code of silence or not, but Hanna took the initiative and told me her sister's name was Rebecca. I thanked Hanna. Then I explained to Rebecca that I needed some quick lessons on how to drive the horses and how much easier it would be if she verbalized those instructions. I promised her that Hanna and I wouldn't tell anyone. She looked at me trying to decide what to do. Hanna and I both crossed our hearts in solidarity to keep Rebecca's secret. Rebecca smiled and agreed.

"Rebecca explained the horses already knew we were going back to the house and were well trained in where to go and what to do. All I had to do was walk behind them and hold the reins off the ground, so they didn't get tangled. I learned *get up* makes them go and *whoa* stops them. *Gee* means go left and *haw* means go right. Saying *back-back* makes them back up. They are draft horses, I learned, and only have one speed. They don't trot, run or canter. They walk. They weigh about two thousand pounds each so I should stay out of their way in case they got scared or riled.

"The basket lay where we had left it. Rebecca suggested we should have lunch before we go any further. Hanna and I agreed, so we went over to the shade and opened it up. There were three and a half ham sandwiches, along with some carrots, pickles and four apples. We set the picnic out and ate. We passed the jug of water around and took turns taking swigs.

"It dawned on me that Rebecca and Hanna had been delivering lunches to their father and brother in the field each day. Sending me with

Hanna was a first sign of trusting me. Another small sign that I hadn't considered until now was receiving my lunch sandwich at the outside table by the well and the mother giving me a few minutes to relax during the day after I had eaten.

"After four days my body began to adjust to the heavy work load. My muscles were still sore but not screaming as loud. My life on the farm was all work. I saw no playtime. I took comfort in that little bit of camaraderie we shared in the field. I had never really been close to anyone. I had no brothers or sisters and I never knew my dad and my mother had died. I had a bunch of money and no family or true friends. I began to envy this family.

"All at once Rebecca gathered up the basket. We took one last drink of water and she dumped the rest out. There was no use carrying it back to the house.

"She told me to take her father's team and follow her. She got behind the other team and put the reins in her hand. With one last look to reassure herself that I was ready she yelled, 'Get up.' Her team started to move. My team did not move. I was about to open my mouth when Hanna yelled, 'Get up.' The team started walking.

"My horses followed the other team. We arrived at the barn with no problems. They walked right up behind the first team and stopped all by themselves. I looked at Rebecca and she gave me the thumbs up. I decided the horses would have walked behind the other team whether I was back there or not.

"Rebecca went into the house but quickly returned. She said we would have to do all the chores since the others were gone. It was late afternoon, so all the regular end-of-day chores needed to be done. I knew the drill on the watering so she concentrated on other responsibilities. The seven-year-old girl came out and she and Hanna fed the chickens and ducks. I grabbed the water buckets and began the trips back and forth between the pump and all the water receptacles. Rebecca began unharnessing both teams of horses and organizing the straps in the barn as her brother normally did. Even though the horses didn't work as long as usual they had stood outside in the sun all day. There was a lot to do, so we all pitched in.

"By the time we finished, it was getting dark. As we headed up to the house, I saw the table near the well set up for eating. The young married woman had taken up the task to get our supper ready. I had seen her husband and the older boy come home. The older boy came out to the barn and took over brushing the horses so Rebecca helped me finish up.

"Rebecca motioned me to come with her. We went to the well and washed up. The men went inside and the two little girls were already sitting at the outside table. It had four plates on it. I walked up to the table and Hanna patted the seat beside her. I looked at Rebecca and she smiled and nodded. I sat beside Hanna and gave her a little hug.

"Rebecca sat down and bowed her head. The other two followed suit. I looked down as she said grace. When she finished, we passed around the bowls of food. This group had a long hard day and managed to step up and get everything done. We carried our plates inside, washed and dried them, then put them away. We all went to bed.

"I heard the buggy pull up shortly after we were in bed, but no one got up to see what had happened, so I didn't either. Hanna had fallen asleep. She always fell asleep first. As she slept, she continued to thrash around and kicked me in the side. I didn't mind it. Sleeping with her was calming, especially when she snuggled up against me.

"Morning came early. I was adjusting to getting up before dawn. Rebecca got up and I followed her downstairs and outside for our morning chores. She motioned to the feed and she grabbed the milking buckets. Losing the young boy added to our workload. That's when I realized I had only been there five days. Before I arrived, Rebecca was doing all the work alone. I needed to step it up again.

"To my surprise, Jonathon came into the barn and gathered Rebecca and the two young girls and me. He said Isaac had a broken leg and would be in bed a few days before he could get up but everything would be fine. He kept it short and sweet but we knew what was going on. At least I learned the young boy's name.

"When we finished the chores, we headed into the house for breakfast. I saw nine plates as usual and went to the cupboard to get mine. Jonathon stood at his place and motioned me over to him. I looked down keeping my eyes on the floor and went to his side. He reached behind and presented me with a new head bonnet, one with a blue ribbon around it. I was amazed at the gift. He told everyone that Isaac would be eating in his room. As he sat down, the family all sat in their places. There was an open seat with a plate on it beside Hanna. She beamed as she patted the seat beside her. I looked at Jonathon. He smiled a little and nodded his head. I didn't look at anyone but could tell they were all watching. I sat down beside Hanna and lowered my head. Jonathon said grace and they passed the food around.

"The food was distributed with Jonathon taking his portion first then he passed the bowl to his wife. There was a pecking order to the food. I had observed it from the other room. Hanna was the smallest so she got the last portion. After the mom, the food goes to the young man and his wife then to the young man who left every day. Then Rebecca the other young girl and down eventually to Hanna. I was sitting last behind Hanna but at least I was at the table.

"By the time it got to me there wasn't much left in each bowl. The mother noticed how little I had and she got up and brought the bread and butter to the table as well as a bowl of fruit. She was watching out for me. I was grateful.

"To my surprise Jonathon looked at me and said, 'Alexandria, this is my family.' He pointed to his wife and said her name was Martha, then sons Mark and Abram. He pointed to the married girl and introduced her as Ruth, Mark's wife. Pointing to the three girls and he called out Rebecca, Mary and Hanna. I looked and smiled a little at each one. They all nodded to acknowledge me.

"Jonathon had broken the code of silence. Since it was still a little awkward, he began by telling everyone what he expected of them that day. When he finished the list, he told everyone the family was lucky that I had been at the accident yesterday. The doctor told him I had done everything right in the field. My eyes may have been focused on the floor as he spoke, but inside I was beaming."

I couldn't help but see how the simple act of explaining that moment affected Alexandria's demeanor. She was still beaming. "That must have made you feel good compared to the first few days with the Yoder family," I said.

Her smile grew. "Mr. Woods, I was flying high knowing I would be able to talk to everyone. I understood talking to the males was still a need-to-speak basis but I had seen the women chatting as they worked, except when I came around. I had so many questions to ask Rebecca and was sure she wanted to talk as well. With the amount of work there was to complete, sharing some thoughts would help pass the time. It was the best meal I had ever eaten."

TWELVE

"Over the next few weeks, I learned a lot about the Amish way of life. My main source of information was Rebecca since we were together most of the time. With Isaac laid up, all of his chores were now divided among the rest of us.

"I learned that Mark and Abram went to a construction job each day. They walked two miles where several men gathered and were picked up by a van driver and taken to work. Since they were gone eleven hours a day, they only did chores at home when necessary.

"Mark was Jonathon's oldest son. He and Ruth had been married for two years and both were twenty years old. They lived in the back part of the house and had a six-month-old daughter named Grace. Next were Abram who was seventeen and Rebecca at fifteen. Isaac was twelve and Mary was eight. That left four-year-old Hanna. They all lived and worked together in one house.

"At twelve, Isaac was on the brink of being treated like a man. He didn't take it well when he was propped up at the kitchen table a few days into his recovery and made to peel potatoes and any other chores that could be done sitting down, most of which revolved around cooking. After a week he was able to get to the barn and quickly reclaimed the morning and evening milking duties from Rebecca. It only took a half hour each time, but it really helped to take that off our list of duties.

"The huge garden took so much time to maintain. There was always something that needed done. I learned they canned enough produce to get them through the winter and sold the excess. We had been eating canned vegetables from last summer and the stock was getting low. We had corn, green beans, peas, tomatoes, potatoes and all kinds of jams and jellies. The pantry was like a mini grocery store. As the plants began to grow in the garden, I understood how their winter meals depended on how much was grown during the summer. This was not some gardening hobby. This was to feed the family.

"The family routine was the same every day except Saturday night and Sunday. Saturday night was bath night. Being last at the table also meant being last in the bath tub. We had worked hard all week and other then a few wipes with a wash rag or washing faces at the well, we were all filthy. The guys went first one after the other. They bathed in the same water. I was relieved the water was changed when they were done. The only problem was I was last in the girl's line and we were just as dirty as the guys. By the time I got in the tub it looked like I was bathing in chocolate milk. The water was cool and pieces of grass, dirt, and other debris floated on the surface. Since I was last, I dumped the water out when I was finished and washed the ring of dirt from the tub. As bad as it was, bathing in dirty water was better than not bathing. Martha was kind enough to give me a second dress so I had something clean to wear.

"Amish families don't work on Sundays. Twice a month they attend church and the other Sundays they spend visiting nearby families. Animals still have to be fed and watered and the cows milked but beyond that everyone takes the day off. My first two weeks with the family, Martha stayed home with me on Sunday. She sat outside sewing and knitting, while I played with the animals and relaxed. It was a day of rest. On the second Sunday I found out how I ended up at their home instead of another detention center or worse.

"Martha explained when her son Abram left the community for rumspringa last year, he traveled to Long Island where he fell in with a group of teenagers and started drinking alcohol. He got in trouble with the law and was brought before Judge Mark. Even though it was unusual, Jonathon went before Judge Mark to ask if Abram could be released into his custody. Abram told his father and the judge that he was ready to commit to the Amish faith. Abram was given probation and one hundred hours of community service to be completed within the Amish community. Judge Mark drove out a couple of times to check on Abram. On the second trip, Jonathon invited him to share a meal with the family. Not as a family member but as a guest."

I noticed a slight smile and twinkle in her eyes. "I don't get it. Why are you smiling?"

"I can't help but laugh every time I think about Judge Mark sitting at the end of the table like me. On his last visit, Jonathon voiced his appreciation for the kindness shown to his family. Mark responded that someday he might need a favor from Jonathon. Martha told me the thought of an Amish man helping a big city judge made both men laugh out loud that day.

"Then one day, Judge Mark showed up to collect that favor. 'That is the only reason you are here with us today,' Martha explained. 'And I am so glad you are here.' I hugged her for almost a minute. I felt so close to her. Even my mother had never shown me this kind of love. I knew then I never wanted to leave.

"The next Sunday, they left me home by myself. I missed the other girls after only thirty minutes. They were gone for hours."

"But you finally had some time to yourself. Did you enjoy the afternoon? Before Alexandria could respond, my attention moved to the blank spot in my notes. My pen had stopped writing and shaking it wasn't helpful. "Sorry, give me a second." Reaching into my desk for another pen, I tested it, then asked, "Did you take a nap? What did you do?"

"No, I did not take a nap," she almost smiled at my question. "The time alone gave me a chance to reflect on my old life. There are so many people around me all the time, but they don't really know me nor do they care about me. It's all about the shows and making money. By living without a lot of luxuries the Amish don't need much money, but they are truly appreciative of what they do have, especially their family.

"I began to understand the meaning of the words *rat race*. You work hard to buy stuff, but when you get it, you see more stuff so you work harder to get that stuff. Then someone else has different stuff and you want that stuff, too. You're always buying the latest and greatest clothes or gadgets even though there's nothing wrong with what you already have.

You're just trying to keep up with everyone else. Cell phones and computers are the worst. As soon as you get one, an even better one comes out. Your friends talk about what they bought, then suddenly you've got to have the same thing. It is such a trap. Young kids ask their parents to buy things and expect the parents to do it, which they usually do. Today, most twelve-year-old kids have a cell phone. Why? Two months ago, I couldn't imagine being without my cell phone or computer for just a few minutes. I've survived without them for almost four months. There is no one I need or want to call anyways. I fell into this family life even though it was hard work. It feels great to be part of a team.

"During breakfast on the fourth Saturday, Jonathan announced we were all going into town after lunch. Hanna told me the family doesn't make the trip very often. We hurried to finish our chores. After lunch we climbed into the wagon. I didn't know where we were going but didn't care because it was my first time off the farm since I arrived. It was a beautiful sunny day. The wagon was normally used in the field so there was no top on it. Hanna sat on my lap as we rode. It was a five-mile ride into a small nearby town. The girls went into a fabric store and the men went down the street to the hardware store. We looked at the bolts of fabric with all their patterns and colors. It was nice to see all the options, but in the end Martha bought a few yards of the same blue fabric that all their other clothes were made from.

"Since the hardware store was only a couple of blocks away, we started walking to the wagon. About halfway there, three teenage boys rode by on their bicycles, yelling something about hot babes. We kept our gaze to the ground and didn't reply. They decided to harass us, blocking our way so we stood there with our heads down. Our subservient attitudes only emboldened them more as they proceeded to ask if they could look under our dresses. One was bigger than me and the other two were my size. The biggest boy reached down and grabbed Rebecca's dress pulling it up a little before she jerked away from him. My blood boiled. Without thinking I grabbed him by the throat and punched him in the stomach. He went down. I then raced over to the other one and kicked him in the groin. He went down also. I looked at the third one who threw up his hands in surrender and ran away."

My mouth dropped open at hearing this young demure girl explain how she had beat up two boys and scared off a third. "Remind me not to make you mad," I said jokingly. "Where were the men while you were teaching these guys a lesson?"

"The men came out of the hardware store in time to see the kick to the groin and the third boy ride away in surrender. They ran up fast, just as the two got to their feet. I was in a defensive posture and ready if the boys came at me or the other women. I didn't think they would but I was ready. They didn't see Jonathon coming. He grabbed both boys from behind and dangled them from his arms. He was a big scary man. They wiggled their legs trying to escape. He shook them hard causing them to stop and hang there limp. You could tell Jonathon was furious. He brought them both around and was face to face with them, still holding them off the ground. One tried to say something but only managed to mumble a couple of incoherent words. Jonathon screamed in his face, 'SHUT UP.' I thought he was going to kill them. Then after a second or two he slowly lowered them to the ground. He released them and in a very deep voice said, 'Now get.' They immediately ran. They were so scared they forgot their bikes.

"Jonathon pointed to the wagon and we all walked to it and got in. No one said anything on the way home. When we got home, Jonathan told me to wait at the table near the pump. He spoke to Martha then sent her inside. Everyone else was already inside the house.

"After he unhitched the horse, he came to the table by the well. He wanted an explanation. Keeping my eyes to the ground, I told him how the boys harassed us and we just ignored them but when one of them actually grabbed Rebecca's dress, I lost control. I told him when I made videos for the internet, we did things and taped them and then charged subscribers to watch them. As Alexandria I had done the first aid video series. As Alex I took self-defense classes for two years and earned a brown belt. I apologized for losing control and said it would never happen again. I kept my eyes down and went silent. There was no excuse for my actions.

"Jonathon asked if I realized there were three of them and I could have been hurt. I shook my head. I didn't think, just reacted. He then asked if I remembered the hen from my first day at their farm and how it risked everything for her chicks and him telling me he would protect his family at all costs. I nodded. He said, 'I try to teach my children that violence is not the way.' He turned toward the house and walked inside. I followed him.

"When we went inside the supper table was ready. Everyone was already seated which was odd. Jonathon went to the head of the table and sat at his place. The rest of the family looked a little out of place. I went to my spot by Hanna and saw she was sitting all the way at the end of the table. There was no place setting for me. My eyes welled at the thought of losing my spot because of those dumb boys. I screwed up by losing control. I had shamed them.

"I went to the cupboard to get my plate when I looked up and noticed everyone was looking at me. Their expressions were different from what I had witnessed since my arrival. As I scanned across the table my eyes met Rebecca's and she patted the seat beside her. Between her and Isaac was an empty place setting. This position at the table was where a girl in the family of my age should sit. I looked at Jonathon and he said, 'Sometimes we need to be a hen.' All at once I realized that I was being welcomed into the family as one of their own. I burst into tears and so did all the other females. I sat down next to Rebecca, sniffling and wiping my tears away. I bowed my head and for the first time in my life thanked God for the new family he had given me.

"Over the next three months, I fell right in with the family, embracing every aspect of my new life. No one had ever cared for me like this before. Everyone works extremely hard each day just to make it. As the days passed, I found my own routine within the family. Not much stops us from our assigned tasks. Hanna, being the smallest, feeds the chickens and ducks. Her job is to spread the chicken feed on the ground so they have an area to feed. It isn't a hard job but needs to be done.

"One morning I came out of the barn with full water buckets and heard Hanna screaming. One of the roosters was attacking her. She kicked and swung her corn pail, but the rooster was relentless. It ran up on her flapping its wings and trying to claw its way up her dress. I ran and picked her up in my arms, but the rooster came after me. I kicked it away, but it kept charging at us.

"That's when Rebecca came out of the barn. She ran to the rooster and grabbed it by the neck. She made a swift upwards motion while holding the rooster and then a hard downward motion. Almost like she was chopping wood. At the bottom of the downward motion, she yanked it up again, hard and fast. When she stopped, the lifeless rooster hung in her hands. Hanna and I had witnessed the brutal ringing of its neck. Seeing that everything was calm Rebecca told me to finish as much of the chores as I could and that she would deal with the rooster situation. That's when she turned and asked Hanna if she wanted chicken soup or fried chicken for supper. With her little finger pointing at the dead rooster Hanna exclaimed in a loud voice, 'FRIED.' With that answer Rebecca grabbed another rooster by its legs and walked around behind the barn.

"I had never seen anything like that in my life. It seemed unfair that the second rooster lost its life because the first one had attacked Hanna. Then it became clear, if we were having fried chicken for supper, the large family demanded additional food for the table. I set Hanna down and she grabbed her bucket and went back into the barn to get more feed like nothing had happened. This family was a tough bunch. Another reminder of how I needed to step it up.

"Thirty minutes later, I saw Rebecca go into the house carrying two chicken carcasses. That night I wasn't sure if I could eat the chicken I had seen slaughtered. But as the platter passed by me at supper, the fried chicken smelled amazing and I helped myself to a thigh. As the first bite melted in my mouth any thoughts of skipping supper vanished. No one thought anything about the events of earlier. To them it was just another day.

"We all depend on each other to get the farm work done. I have a great sense of pride when I think about being a contributing member of the team. We grow all our own food. We are self-sufficient in almost every way. If anyone in the community needs help, everyone volunteers. For the first time in my life, I have people who truly love and care for me."

Alexandria sat back in the chair, completely relaxed with the most serene expression I've ever seen. Now it was my turn to lead the conversation. "So, where do my services fit into this scenario you find idyllic but that many would call difficult, seeing only harsh living conditions and hard work?" We had discussed the basics previously, but I needed to be sure of her intent.

She turned serious once again and looked me straight in the eye. "I want to abandon my old life and never look back. I considered just disappearing but that wouldn't be the right thing to do. I need to button up my old life and leave it behind forever. It will not be easy because of my followers and my guardian but it needs to happen. How do we make it happen, Mr. Woods?"

Laying the pen and legal pad aside, I said, "Normally, becoming emancipated is not that tough if no one protests and you have enough assets to sustain yourself, but I'm pretty sure Jeremy won't let you go without a fight." My research showed Jeremy starting over with another girl was not an option. He tried several others, and they just didn't take off. His success had brought copycats onto the internet and launching someone else would not bring in the money Alexandria created. He would not let his golden goose go uncontested.

I had a lot to think through before I could file court papers. There were only two weeks until Mark's temporary custody ended. I assured Alexandria I would be working on her case all week to complete a plan of action before the deadline. If we did not file anything by her return date, Mark would have questions to answer and she would be considered a runaway. Not a good start towards being emancipated. I asked if we could meet again to go over what I come up with. She said she would be here at 6:00 A.M. Friday morning. At this point I did not need or want to know where she was living. I could still claim ignorance and avoid committing a crime.

She reminded me about being glad Mark sent her to me and was happy to have me as her champion. By adding that title, she placed more pressure on my already growing fears. I had no idea how to make this happen without everything turning into a zoo. I knew as soon as I filed on her behalf the frenzy would start. The reporters would swarm in to try and find her. My current life would be over.

She stood up and I walked her to the front door. "One last request if possible?" she asked. "I am praying we can keep where I live and who I live with a secret. They don't want any publicity and wouldn't welcome outsiders poking into their lives, asking questions and snapping photos." I told her I would do my best. As she walked out the door she said cheerfully, "See you Friday."

The door closed and I considered the week in front of me. Then I thought about Alexandria's week. Sure, she had a lot of work to do but her work would not be stressful. At the end of the day, she would lay her tired head down on her pillow and get a good night's sleep. Content with where she lives and the passions she has. Not really a bad life to have. I on the other hand, haven't had a good night's sleep since I met her.

THIRTEEN

I emailed Mark, asking him to call me. I was all in and hoped he had a plan. If she became a runaway, we could both be considered accessories to helping a fugitive. Since it was still early, I closed my computer and walked down the street to my regular restaurant and had my normal breakfast. The same place where I had eaten breakfast for years. The waitress knew what to bring me. I am a creature of habit. Pretty boring by most people's standards.

Mark didn't call back, but at 9:15, the normal time for an attorney or judge to get to work, I received an email from him with a large attachment. I opened it and started reading his plan of how he would proceed if he were handling her case. He had been thinking about this for a long time. I was glad to have his input.

Since the timeframe was limited, and court cases could take up to ninety days, he wanted me to contact Alexandria's guardian, Jeremy, and see if he would sign an extension giving Mark custody over Alexandria for no more than one more month. I was not to tell him of her plans but come up with something that would get him to sign. I was not as good at mind games as Mark, but I thought it was worth a try. I knew as soon as I contacted him, the hunt for Alex would be on. Jeremy had not heard a thing from Alex in over three and a half months. She was supposed to get out after four months on good behavior. Jeremy's attorney had contacted Mark who said she would not be released after four months but did not give any details as to what had happened.

I dialed his number and he picked up on the fourth ring. "Hi, Jeremy. This is Ronald Woods from Woods Law Office in Pennsylvania. I was asked by Mark Thomas, a colleague of mine, to call you about Alex Andres. Do you have a minute to talk?"

His response was immediate. "Yes."

"Jeremy, we are all trying to get Alex released next week as originally planned, but there has been a snag. Judge Thomas has a problem with the timeline. Do you remember the original deal that if violated he would send her to jail for three years?"

Barely audible, he claimed to remember.

I continued. "Well, he does not want that to happen. Alexandria has requested to stay four more weeks, but the judge's temporary custody expires next week. If you would be willing to extend that order for no more than four additional weeks Alexandria should be free to go by then. The problem is she will not be ready next week. Can we make this happen so we can avoid any other problems?"

He delayed a second and then asked, "Who is this again?"

I explained and gave him my contact information when he asked if he could call me back. Just before we hung up, I said, "I don't know where the girl is at but I understand she is a high-profile case and Mark wants this to stay private for now."

He said he would call me by the end of the day.

At 1:00 that afternoon, my phone rang. Jeremy asked, "Is there a guarantee she will be released in four weeks?"

"No. The only thing for sure is Alexandria will not be coming back to your place in two weeks."

There was a short pause before he finally consented to thirty more days of temporary guardianship. "Can I talk to her?"

"Jeremy, as I said earlier, I don't know where she is and have no way to get a hold of her." I was walking a thin line. Technically, I was telling the truth, just maybe not all of it.

We agreed I would draw up the papers and send them over to his attorney's office and he promised to have them signed and sent back within one day. At least that gave us another month before custody of Alexandria became an issue.

Once again, I emailed Mark and informed him of my success with Jeremy. I asked about the next part of the plan. I don't know what I was expecting, but found myself staring at my email, waiting for a response. Since my email address had become popular in the last two weeks, I decided to clean out my inbox. So many emails, so many people trying to scam me. It would be funny except for the fact that real people still fall for this stuff and are scammed into losing their hard-earned money. A promise of loads of free money just seems to suck them in.

Mark's email showed up just after noon. I knew he had regular court hours, and this was not the only matter he was dealing with, but it was the biggest case I had ever handled. The message started out congratulating me on getting the extension and proceeded to tell me what I already knew about getting someone emancipated. He recommended filing her motion as soon as possible. Since she had been in this state for over three months, he also recommended getting her a post office box and changing her residence status to Pennsylvania which meant the case would be heard in this state and county instead of New York where Jeremy lives.

I had not seen that coming but it made good sense to keep it here. Normally, these things are decided by a judge and a case worker if a party wants to protest the emancipation. It would be a lot harder to convince a judge in this state that living on a farm in rural Pennsylvania is bad for her. People in New York might consider us backwards and the Amish as downright crazy, but anyone around here will be sympathetic to her request.

He also recommended having her take the GED ASAP. If she passed, which I figured she would, it could eliminate any questions on her having to attend school. I sent an email to my assistant to investigate the GED test, so we could get that rolling. I would not see Alexandria until Friday, giving us time to look it up.

I knew Jeremy had already Googled me and found out I was a nobody in the legal field. I also knew he would hire a private investigator to follow me. He had been trying to find Alex for three and half months and came up empty. My contacting him was his first lead on her whereabouts. Even though I had told him I didn't know where she was, he would send someone to check me out. They would find a boring local attorney. After a few days of watching me eat at the diner and go home early, they'll give up.

The papers Jeremy signed showed up on Tuesday by FedEx, all notarized and legal. The extension was done. We had bought Alexandria at least four more weeks. I decided to wait on filing her petition for emancipation until after she had taken the GED, just in case the media found out her location and ruined everything. I also decided to get her a post office box in the next county. We have a large Amish community in our county, so I was fairly certain she was within twenty miles of my office, but you never know. I had not seen her dropped off or picked up. I know sometimes the Amish pay people with vans and trucks to transport them to places. If that's the case, she could be living two states away.

My assistant, Brenda, found a GED test being given in two weeks at a local college. It was not required but highly recommended that you take a refresher course first. I suppose if you had dropped out of school and wanted to take the test a few years later a refresher would be warranted, but Alexandria has been in a private tutoring situation. I decided to order the refresher book with overnight shipping so I could give it to her on Friday.

A post office box in another city can be reserved online by filling out Form 1583 to reserve the box. However, to use it you must travel to that post office and present two forms of identification to activate the mailbox and start receiving mail. Alexandria probably would not have two forms of ID with her on Friday. I decided to man up and accept the fact that the press and all the headhunters would be knocking at my door soon enough. I walked down to the post office a block from my office and asked for an application to rent a box. At least it would be easier to access.

I did my research and prepared the documents to file Alexandria's emancipation. If the judge agreed, she could be on her own right away. If not, Jeremy would remain her guardian. It looked like I could put together a good case to discredit any claim he had as legal guardian. Her grandmother had signed her over to him, but did she have the mental capacity to do so at the time? That could be another case for the judge to decide. The last thing I wanted to happen was for her to become a ward of the state, which meant a foster home. The foster care people try their best. Little kids who are placed have a shot at a normal life, but teenagers who have been in trouble are more difficult to place in long-term homes. Of course, her being an internet star would change everything.

FOURTEEN

I arrived at my office at 5:55 A.M. on Friday. Just enough time to snap on the lights before Alexandria showed up at 6:00 A.M. She arrived right on time wearing a long-sleeve, flowered dress that went all the way to her shoes. This time she also had a scarf covering her head.

We exchanged hellos as she removed the scarf. "How was your week?"

"Great," she responded with a smile.

I cannot remember the last time I had a great week. There is a lot of pressure in my job. Clients think I should be able to wave a magic wand and make all their troubles disappear. Most of the time the problems were created by the clients themselves. I spent the week trying to button up some of my current cases, so for the first time ever I was not taking on anything new. I figure once the news gets out on Alexandria's case, I won't have much time for anything else.

I started the session by explaining our progress, including extending Mark's guardianship. I told her about spotting a man following me the same day I had talked to Jeremy and how I would not have noticed him if I wasn't looking for him. After forty-eight hours of watching my dull life, he disappeared. All had gone well on that part of the plan.

We discussed her taking the GED and I gave her the refresher guide I had ordered. She assured me she was an excellent student and should not have any problems passing the test. The only issue we had was presenting her ID at the testing site. I decided I would request it be sent via Mark.

Since they had taken her personal effects at the police station during processing, they should have her ID.

Her next appointment was set for the Saturday of the test at our usual 6:00 A.M. time slot. That would give us plenty of time to get to the testing site by 9:00 A.M. She planned to dress as she does during our meetings. That way she would be seen as a shy introvert and not expected to interact with anyone. If no one realized who she was during registration she might get in and out without being recognized

The next week was spent wrapping up my other open cases. As soon as I filed her motion I would be tied up for the foreseeable future. Since we had agreed to wait until she had taken the GED to start anything all I had to do that week on her behalf was get her ID from Mark. All it took was an email to him and it showed up in an overnight envelope the next day. He must have requested her personal items as her guardian.

Saturday came quickly and right at 6:00 A.M. Alexandria walked in my door. I took her over to the post office and we knocked on the door. The postmaster who was a good friend of mine, greeted us and let us in. He locked the door behind us as the post office didn't open until 9:00 A.M. I explained to Alexandria that being in a small town did have some advantages. My friend Allen, the postmaster, agreed to come in early if I bought him breakfast sometime. She presented her ID and an application for a post office box. We paid the $58 yearly fee. She was now a resident of Pennsylvania. Allen did not ask questions.

We then drove the forty miles to the community college to get her registered for the test. As we drove, I asked how her week had gone. She was a little nervous about the test but said she had read the entire prep textbook and did the practice test. If she wasn't recognized she thought it should go well.

Since it was late summer, she had been going to the farmers market to help sell the family's extra vegetables. She said she had gotten good at keeping her head down and not speaking much around other people. If someone persisted and tried to speak with her, she politely told them she didn't speak much English. The Amish speak English but also throw in a Germanic dialect that came to be known as Pennsylvania Dutch. All she had to do was say a few sentences in that, even if it didn't make sense, and they would stop asking questions. Another family member also stepped up to take over the transaction. It worked every time.

We decided I would stick around when we got to the college but keep my distance from her. Close enough to hear and see what was going on but far enough away to not look as if we knew each other. If things went south, we planned to run to the car and leave immediately.

Entering the testing building I lagged back. It was recommended that you register early online, but you could register that day. She waited until there were a few people in line. There were three registration lines. Line one was last names beginning with the letters A thru G. Line two was last names H thru O. The last line was for P thru Z. That meant she belonged in line one. A male college student was in charge of the first line. That could be a problem. If he reads her name as he processes her application she could be recognized. I watched as she went to the third line where an elderly lady assisted those registrating. I signaled that she was in the wrong line. She gave me a hard stare that assured me she knew what she was doing, so I moved close enough to hear as she approached.

The lady looked at her ID and told her she needed to go to the first line. Alexandria immediately started to look a little teary eyed and fluttered her eyelids to fight back the tears. The lady immediately noticed her distress and the way she was dressed. She took her aside. "What's the matter, dear?" The woman held Alexandria's shoulder in a consoling manner.

Barely audible, I heard Alexandria say in broken Pennsylvania Dutch, "The men are over there."

Realizing the problem, the woman guided her back over to her desk and told her she would take care of her registration. When Alexandria caught my eye, she winked at me. It amazed me how well she had played the woman without even a plan. Alexandria was one smart cookie.

After registering and paying her test fee, Alexandria went into the testing room with all the other participants. I saw her take a back corner seat near an exit. Those who saw her quickly lost interest and looked away. Little did they know a mega internet star was in their midst. Anyone who recognized her and got her photo would have instant fame and could sell her photo for big bucks. She kept her head down but also watched her surroundings for possible trouble, ready to bolt out of the door if need be.

Alexandria almost jumped out of her seat when a girl came up behind her and asked if she could sit beside her. She nodded her head in assent and the girl sat down. Alexandria assessed the girl quickly and decided she too was a social outcast and just wanted to have someone to sit by.

After about thirty seconds of silence, Alexandria decided to take a chance. Alexandria learned the girl's name was Beth and she had dropped out of school at sixteen. She was now eighteen and needed her GED to take some community college classes. Beth went on to explain she was trying to get her life back on track after some bad choices. "Working fast food is difficult," she explained, not only because of the low pay, but I have to deal with a lot of rude and sometimes, just mean people."

Beth's recounting of some of the things that happened to her at work caused Alexandria to feel bad for her. After all, Alex was responsible for promoting a lot of the bullying currently going on in food establishments. Alexandria wanted to reach out, but couldn't risk saying too much. The girl might recognize her. Just as Beth asked Alexandria about getting her GED an instructor announced it was time to take their seats and settle down. She was thankful she did not have to tell her a lie.

After the test, Alexandria saw Beth waiting for her ride. The girls asked each other about their respective results. Beth felt confident she had passed. Alexandria said the same. Alexandria stepped toward me then turned back and asked Beth if she had her phone and if she wanted to take a photo. Beth excitedly agreed. Alexandria took the selfie with Beth at angle, showing only their faces together. Alexandria handed the phone back to Beth and said, "You'll need money for college. Thank you for your friendship today and I hope you're able to achieve your dream of taking those classes." Alexandria hugged Beth and whispered, "Be sure to post the photo on Facebook with the caption "My new friend, Alexandria." Beth promised to post it ASAP.

As Alexandria reached me, she said, "We better get going." Then she told me what she had done. As her attorney I was pretty upset that she had potentially let the cat out of the bag, but it was going to happen sooner or later. I was just glad it wasn't me. When she registered for her GED, she had put down the new post office box number as her address. Someone was bound to see her name go through, triggering the hunt to track her down.

Beth's circle of friends was small, so it took almost twenty-four hours before someone recognized Alexandria on Beth's Facebook page. That was the first picture of her to surface in four months. The internet lit up with excitement. The first and only lead of where Alex was had finally surfaced. Of course, Beth really didn't know that much but she became instant news. Everyone wanted to interview her. Beth's life had changed forever. Alexandria hoped she had helped her and not made her life a nightmare. The search was on for the lost starlet.

Fifteen

"I plan to file the papers at the courthouse on Monday just after 3:00 P.M.," I said while driving Alexandria back to the office. We made an appointment for the next Saturday, again at 6:00 A.M. "By then the word will be out, so we have to be careful about meeting."

"Why not meet at the farmers market and buy some fresh vegetables on Saturday morning?" she suggested. "You can pass a note to let me know what's happening. Make it look like a grocery list and give it to Jonathon. He'll probably be the biggest guy there."

The market was one town over so I figured that would work. Nothing was going to change in her world unless someone figured out where she was, so I really didn't need to speak to her. I had to admit she was pretty good on the cloak and dagger thing. As she left, I knew Sunday was the last normal day I would have for a long time.

In the next few days, Beth got her fifteen minutes of fame. However, she quickly realized she didn't have much to offer after the original account of their only meeting, so she began making up stories about her and Alexandria and the adventures they shared and what they were planning in the future. No one could prove her wrong and it was news about Alexandria, so the media went with it.

Beth had a complete makeover. The transformation was amazing. Gone was the drab sloppy shy girl. On camera she became a new person. She explained how she and Alexandria had met at the mall and became instant friends. They had discussed Alexandria taking a sabbatical for a while and going a few places together. She wanted to spend a little time to herself and with her best friend.

Jeremy knew the whole thing was a lie, but the internet excitement caused such a surge in activity on both sites he, as any good businessman would, embraced Beth for the time being. Jeremy even had Beth going to Alexandria and Alex's houses, talking about everything they had done. He had her make fifteen-minute videos that cost $1.99 each to watch. Since they were all made-up, there was an unlimited number of stories that Beth could tell, so they produced a bunch of them. The videos started at a place like the zoo or a museum then he would plug in the photo of Beth and Alexandria followed by a few shots of the area and what was at the venue. Beth moderated the scenes and even threw in where and what they ate that day. A few venders validated the stories by saying they were sworn to secrecy about the pair eating at their place. The producers also pulled photos of Alexandria from their archives to add to the experience. Both groups of watchers jumped all over the new videos. The money was flowing again.

On Sunday evening the news broke and so had the fact that Alexandria had an address in my hometown. Reporters flocked from all over the country hoping to get the first picture of the lost star. Jeremy put up a $50,000 reward for the whereabouts of Alex. Bounty hunters as well as fans all decided they wanted to be part of the search. All the local hotels and Airbnbs were fully booked. Nearby towns were also overrun.

Luckily, word had not gotten out that I was involved. The only one who knew that was Jeremy. Sunday night at 6:00 P.M. I saw a familiar car parked on my street. My tail had returned. I knew the answering machine at work would have a message from Jeremy. I decided to stay home and watch television alone for one last night.

The next morning, I went to my regular diner to find it completely packed with a line of people waiting to get in. My friend Allen, the postmaster, saw me and signaled me to come in and sit with him. I gladly accepted. The waitress ran past me and nodded. My order was placed.

As I sat down Allen was grinning. "Can I assume you had something to do with all this chaos?"

I nodded in the affirmative. "My life will change at 9:00 A.M. after I arrive at the office, so if we could have a normal conversation, I would appreciate it."

"A group of reporters have stationed themselves at the post office already," he said.

I had not realized it, but his day and week wouldn't be any better with people hounding him for Alexandria's address. The bill for his breakfast lay next to his plate. With a knowing look, he slid it over to me. I acquiesced and put it beside my placemat. Not sure where they got the idea, but the fans thought they could walk into the post office and request anyone's address. No one even thought about privacy issues. It became obvious I would be buying Allen's breakfast again.

We sat and listened to the conversations around us. From what we could hear, there were a lot of reporters in the diner. Also, a lot of fans. My normal breakfast came in record time. I figured the cook had fried up a bunch of the normal breakfast items ahead and since mine was bacon, eggs and hash browns he just had to throw them on the plate. I appreciated the quick service, but was in no hurry to get to my office. I ate slowly and chatted with Allen about the weather and the local sports news.

At 8:45 I left the diner and walked to my office. There was a car parked in front with two guys sitting in it. As I unlocked the door, they got out and followed me in. We did not speak. I pointed to the reception area, and they headed in and sat down. I knew who they were and what they wanted. I flipped on the lights, taking my time to check everything, start my computer, and say a little prayer. A few minutes later, I figured I might as well get it over with.

The two guys out front kept peering around the corner to see if I was coming to get them or just leaving them there. I wondered, *Do these guys think I'll produce Alexandria on demand; snap my fingers and have her step out of the closet.* Knowing they would show up, I had all weekend to devise a plan. My assistant Brenda walked in on schedule, and I asked her to show them into the conference room. It was only an extra office with a table and a few chairs where ten people could conduct business like signing the documents to buy a house or finalize a divorce.

Brenda showed them in, asked them to sit down and offered coffee or water. They declined. I walked in with my pad and pen ready to take notes if needed. I shook hands with both men and introduced myself.

One was Jeremy and the other was his attorney, Tom Dugan. "What can I do for you, today?" I asked.

Jeremy started as I thought he would, demanding I produce Alex before the end of business. I repeated that I didn't know where she was. To which he responded, "I don't believe you and will see you brought up on criminal charges if she isn't delivered today."

I calmly looked him right in the eye and said, "I think you both need to leave right now."

"We're not going anywhere without her," Jeremy said.

"Brenda, please call the sheriff and ask him to come over. I have two trespassers that need to be escorted out."

Tom Dugan, the lawyer, said we needed to talk. I told him we did not. As far as I was concerned, she was a minor and I would be in trouble if I discussed anything about her with him.

Jeremy was angry and not above raising his voice. "I am her guardian and I will file criminal charges against you."

Just as planned, I stood and walked to the conference room door before turning around. "You are NOT her legal guardian right now. You have NO right to know anything about where she is and what she is doing. The only one I can discuss her personal matters with is Judge Mark Thomas. He is her legal guardian right now." Their mouths both dropped. They realized they had been played. They had no legal standing as far as Alexandria was concerned for the near future.

As if on cue the sheriff came through the front door. "Sheriff, I asked these men to leave, and they refused. Please escort them out and inform them if they come in again, I will file trespassing and harassment charges against them."

The sheriff was a younger man, but stoutly built. He turned so they could not see and winked at me. Then he depressed his shoulder mic and spoke into it. "All units, I need backup at Ronald Woods' office."

Jeremy and his attorney both raised their hands in surrender. They may be big shots in their town but both knew that didn't mean a thing here. If they caused trouble they would be thrown in jail. They quickly walked past me and out of the door. The sheriff pressed his mic and said, "Cancel that assistance. All units stand down." He had already been to the post office and talked to Allen. Living in a small town does have it perks.

<hr/>

Anthony Richards, our local judge, is a great guy. Unfortunately for him, he was about to be dragged into this also. I had not thought about how all of this would affect our whole community. The local shops and eateries were experiencing a boom in business, but local services were being stretched to their maximum. Kind of like what happens to a vacation town when their population quadruples each summer. The difference being, they know what's coming and prepare for it. Our little community was not prepared for an extra ten thousand people showing up in less than twenty-four hours with more on the way. All these people were here looking for Alex. They had no idea there was about to be another explosion.

I went to the courthouse to file my papers for Alexandria's emancipation at 1:00 P.M., asking if I could have a quick word with the judge to bring him up to speed. He was not a happy camper to learn what I had just filed. Since he knows me well, he felt obliged to ask, "What were you thinking taking this case, Ronald?" I just told him she needed my help.

Thirty days is the normal amount of time it takes to get on the court docket, but since we are in a small town and Judge Richards was already seeing the results of the pending case, he set the preliminary hearing for the next Monday at 10:00 A.M.

We agreed his ruling would take longer than the two weeks left on Mark's guardianship, so the court would also send Jeremy notice of the court proceedings. The endgame would be exposed. Alexandria would have her day in court, but Jeremy would also be there to fight it.

Over the next two days our little town was completely overrun with tourists. The Beth videos had encouraged the hunt and the hope of a $50,000 reward. Now, with the news of her address being in our small town, things went from bad to worse. Overnight accommodations were fully booked so people resorted to campgrounds and even tents in our local parks. The local gas station ran out of gas, and there was no bottled water to be found anywhere. The grocery store looked like they were hit by a natural disaster with all the empty shelves. Word got around among the locals that I had brought all this down upon them, causing a lot of hard stares to be thrown in my direction, but I stayed out of the bullseye of the horde. Jeremy had not leaked the news about the upcoming court case, meaning everyone was just hanging around town hoping to run into Alexandria.

By Saturday, the local Amish community decided to bring their farmer's market here with so many visitors in town. They sold their produce and other products, offering everything from their gardens and fruit trees as well as honey, homemade laundry soap, and baked goods.

I spotted a large man, surmised it was Jonathon and quickly wrote out a note. When viewed from a distance, it looked like a shopping list. Knowing Jeremy was having me watched, I walked up to the booth and decided to do a little acting myself. I approached the first girl and asked her as smarmy as I could how she was doing. She looked at me sheepishly, then I asked her name. That sent her retreating and Jonathon approached me. Since I had never met him, he assumed I was just another jerk harassing his daughter. With a booming voice he asked what I needed.

Anyone watching would not have wanted to be me. I shrank back and handed him my list. He grabbed it and stepped over by the vegetables. As he began to read it, he realized it was a note to Alexandria telling her about the Monday court date and she would not need to attend. I did not need to see her on Friday. I asked if a Tuesday meeting for an update would work for her.

As I watched him read it, he called a girl over to fill my order. I was amazed when I realized it was Alexandria. Tagging along beside her was a young girl I assumed was Hanna. As Alexandria walked along, she would check the list and hand the items to Hanna who was carrying the bag. She appeared to be checking off items as she went down the list. Ten thousand people looking for her and she was right here in front of them. Granted, she wore a long dress and a bonnet that covered almost all her face, but she was right here. She was careful not to look me in the eye. I guess the old saying that the best place to hide is in plain view.

Finally, she stopped putting items in the bag and handed it to Jonathon. He brought it over and gruffly told me my total was $19. I was a bachelor. What was I going to do with $19 worth of produce, but how could I argue? I looked over at Alexandria and caught a slight smile on her face as she looked away. I paid Jonathon the money and he threw the list into the bag and shoved it back at me. Anyone watching would have been clueless on what had just happened.

As I walked away, I smiled at the fact that Alexandria had just played me. My smile grew wider as I realized I would be billing for my time and the food purchase.

When I got back to my office, I took out the note and read the one-word response, *Okay.*

Sixteen

So far, I had not spoken to Mark. Our email communications were all I had. At this point he was her legal guardian and I was her attorney. We both had our roles to perform. We both had the same goal, but I figured letting him get the same court notice as Jeremy would be the best course of action.

With only two weeks left in Mark's guardianship we all knew Jeremy would be involved in the final hearing. The great part is that for the next two weeks with no legal standing all he can do is observe the proceedings. Since Jeremy had been warned not to come to my office he called and asked to speak to me. Brenda told him I was unavailable and said she would take a message. He asked for me to return his call ASAP. I did not.

It was hard to keep track of my billing time since it consumed all my thoughts, but the legal part was straight forward. Other than taking her to the GED test and getting her post office box I didn't have any other billable miles. There were some minor expenses, but nothing big. I had envisioned hiding her in a hotel with a secret location and dodging reporters. I was beginning to think I would have to look for new clients to cover payroll.

Obviously, Jeremy didn't tell the reporters I was involved, my life—not the town's life—stayed kind of calm. Other than being followed by his private eye everywhere, no one bothered me.

Thursday morning, Brenda informed me of a walk-in asking for a consultation. I wasn't busy and told her to put them in the conference room. I decided to listen to their story before deciding to take on another client.

To my surprise there was a young woman sitting at the conference table. She appeared to be about twenty. She looked familiar but I couldn't place her. I asked if she wanted coffee, but she held up a cup she had brought with her. I recognized it from the coffee shop downtown. Probably not anything close to the coffee I served. As I sat down, I told her my name and asked hers. She said her name was Beth Carson. That's when I recognized her from the GED testing center. She's the girl Alexandria had befriended. Those alarm bells started ringing again. I was aware she was making videos with Jeremy to try to expand her friendship with Alexandria.

Jeremy may not have told the media, but he had at least told her I was involved with Alexandria. I figured Jeremy sent her to negotiate with me on the emancipation filing. The only reason he had not told the press about the case was to keep it quiet. If the fans from the website heard Alexandria and Alex were never coming back, subscriptions would plummet along with his revenue stream. Although this was big news, he needed to keep it under wraps if possible.

Beth was just trying to keep her fifteen minutes of fame alive. She said she would like to meet with Alexandria so they could talk. She pleaded with me. She laid out the case that Alexandria needed to talk to someone her own age. Someone who is a friend. I explained to her that I didn't know where she was, and had no way to reach her at this point. She gave me a snide remark about me not knowing how to reach my own client. I decided to help her out. "If you promise to keep it a secret, I'll give you Alexandria's address." She quickly agreed. I jotted down her post office box number on a sheet of paper and handed it to her. She immediately opened it and read it. Her face dropped as she realized I was playing with her. I told her to write Alexandria a letter and mail it. She picked up her coffee and stomped out in a huff.

I spent the rest of the week and weekend preparing for Monday morning's court appearance. Even though our town was overrun, my world remained quiet. Since Jeremy didn't want the world to know what was going on, I decided to help get the word out. I called my friend Sam, editor of the local newspaper, and told him he needed to be at the courthouse on Monday at 10:00 A.M.

"We don't normally cover courthouse stuff and just write up stories using the transcripts," he said.

I insisted, then said, "You shouldn't tell anyone but make sure you're there."

"What's going on, Ronald?"

"Trust me. You won't regret it."

With all the commotion in town about Alexandria, I think he had an idea who was involved but had no idea of what was transpiring.

I arrived at the courthouse on Monday at 9:55 A.M. No one in the filing office had leaked anything. All was calm there. The world had no idea what was about to happen in this small rural courthouse. All the reporters in town had no idea the scoop of a lifetime was about to happen right under their noses and the local nobody newspaper editor was going to scoop them all.

Entering the courtroom, I saw Jeremy and his attorney sitting on the right side towards the back. We nodded at each other. The only other person in the room was Sam from the newspaper. I gave him a little wave and sat down on the left side. The bailiff and court reporter came in right at 10:00 A.M.

The bailiff announced, "All rise. The Honorable Anthony Richards, presiding," as the judge walked in.

Hearing the words, we all jumped to our feet.

The judge said, "Please be seated." The judge looked around the court and picked up a paper and started reading aloud. "Before me I have court matter 8195764. A request from Alexandria Andres, a minor, who resides in this state. Miss Andres has requested that she be fully recognized by this court and the state of Pennsylvania as an emancipated minor and be fully acknowledged as an adult and oversee all her affairs." He looked up and asked? "Are the interested parties present?"

I glanced back and saw the look on Sam's face as he took out a tablet and frantically scribbled out notes. He was about to be given the scoop of his lifetime.

Standing, I announced, "Ronald Woods, attorney for Miss Andres and representing her in this matter, Your Honor. The judge waved me forward past the barrier separating the gallery from court proceedings and indicated the table to the left. As he instructed, I walked up and set my briefcase on the table.

Jeremy's attorney stood up and introduced himself. "Tom Dugan, Your Honor, representing Jeremy Staley. He is the long-term guardian for Miss Andres." The judge pointed towards the other table and the pair made their way down front and sat down.

"This should not be a complicated case," the judge stated. "A young woman wants to be declared an adult and care for herself. She has a little over a year until she reaches her eighteenth birthday and becomes an adult anyway, so let's lay out the facts to see if she is ready to assume her own guardianship."

He also said his office was contacted by Mark Thomas. "Mr. Thom-has stated he was her temporary guardian, and supports Alexandria being emancipated but understands his guardianship will end before this court issues its findings. He made a request on Miss Andres behalf that she remain at her current location until such time as the court reaches a final decision on this matter.

Jeremy's attorney stood. "Your Honor, my client..."

The judge waved him down. "You will have your chance to speak, Mr. Dugan. Since this is about to become a high-profile case, we are going to go over how it will be handled in my courtroom going forward. I would have preferred to keep this out of the public eye, but I see our local news editor decided to grace us with his presence today, so I can assume he will be reporting on this case as soon as he can." He looked at Sam who nodded in the affirmative. The judge then looked at me and said, "Lucky for him that he just happened to be in the courthouse today. We don't normally get much personal coverage." I nodded in agreement.

The judge continued. "Until last week, I didn't know anything about Miss Andres, who she was or what she does in the online world, nor do I care about that sort of thing. I will be looking at this case solely as a minor petitioning to be emancipated." To Jeremy's attorney he asked, "Is your client planning on supporting this petition?"

Dugan stood, buttoned his suit coat and said, "No, we are not, Your Honor."

The judge looked at his court clerk and asked, "What is the earliest date we can have a hearing?"

As she looked at her calendar Jeremy's attorney raised his hand to be recognized, the judge motioned for him to stand. "We would like to arrange a time to speak with Miss Andres to understand why this is happening? Mr. Staley has not had contact with her for over three months and does not comprehend any of this. Before leaving, she was in good spirits and looking forward to returning."

The judge looked at me, so I stood and stated, "Your Honor, I have been informed by Miss Andres that she does not want to see or talk to Mr. Staley. If you want me to relay a message to her, that can be accommodated. She is not alleging any misconduct by Mr. Staley in anyway. She is simply ready to oversee her own life. She plans on starting over and knows he will not support her in this."

As I sat down Tom Dugan raised his hand again to speak. The judge waved him to sit down and said, "Since Miss Andres has stated in her petition that this has nothing to do with misconduct by her guardian, I will look at the facts and decide if she is ready to be a legal adult. That is all I am here to decide. Is there anything else?"

Mr. Dugan once again raised his hand and the judge nodded at him to continue. He stood and said, "We really do not understand this, Your Honor. She has been gone only three and a half months and now wants to abandon everything she has built. What happened to her? She is acting crazy. We would like to request that she have a mental evaluation."

The judge looked at me then said, "That doesn't seem unreasonable to me. I am ordering that she speak to someone that can explain to me her mental state and reasoning. I need a full understanding of this case to be able to decide why she cannot wait until she is eighteen and becomes a legal adult by age. If this is a publicity stunt, I'll be very upset."

I glanced at Jeremy and saw a small smile cross his face. He had gotten a read on the judge's feelings. Why put everyone through this if in sixteen months it wouldn't matter. I knew why. And in my opinion, she deserves those sixteen months of freedom.

The judge looked at his court clerk as she checked her calendar. Seeing Sam furiously writing, she cleared her throat. "I can set it for a week from Wednesday at 11:00 A.M., if it pleases the court?"

"Good. We're adjourned until Wednesday of next week at 11:00 A.M."

As I stood the judge spoke, "Off the record, I want to say I am not happy with what is going on in our town. There are too many people out there. We cannot accommodate all of them." He then looked at Jeremy and said, "What can be done about this?"

Jeremy shook his head and said, "I have no idea. This is what happens when a celebrity goes missing."

The judge's next statement was for Sam's benefit. He looked at the court reporter and said, "Make sure the court proceedings are made public today promptly at 4:59 P.M."

Suddenly, I had an idea. I looked at Jeremy and said, "Since these people are all looking for her, we might be able to help. Can you have Beth stop by my office tomorrow at 9:00 A.M.? Just her. No one else." Jeremy, sensing a flicker of hope, nodded yes.

As we left, I grabbed Sam's arm and pulled him into a side conference room. I told him he would earn his scoop and sell a bunch of papers in the meantime. I laid out my plan and he agreed. The rest of my night was quiet, while the rest of the town continued to be overrun by fortune seekers.

I went to the farmers market with my list again. This time I brought my own small reusable bag to avoid more produce than I could use.

I approached Jonathan and handed him my list and the bag. He looked at the list and handed it to a girl about Alexandria's age to fill the order. Alexandria slowly walked over and read the list. Once again everyone is out searching and she's standing in plain sight. Without looking at me she nodded her head as she threw in a couple of apples. When my order was complete, I ordered a fruit basket and asked it to be delivered to my office late this afternoon. Jonathan agreed, took my money and returned my bag filled with items from my list, minus a small camera and special edition newspaper which were given to Alexandria and returned to me later. The fruit basket was delivered by two of the older Amish women, and my plan was ready.

SEVENTEEN

Beth was waiting for me when I arrived at my office at 8:30 the next morning. Her excitement grew with the expectation of seeing Alexandria. She would not. Beth's story had pretty much run its course and she needed to make herself relevant again. When I came into the conference room she asked where Alexandria was. I told her she wasn't coming. Her disappointment was obvious.

"I need your help," I told her. "You'll get something in return, but you must agree not to divulge this to anyone except Jeremy." Since she had nothing to lose, she agreed. I handed her a copy of our local paper that had a headline that read "Me and my BFF are going on vacation." Alexandria was holding the paper and smiling for the camera.

Beth's face lit up. "When are we leaving?"

I told her it wasn't exactly like that and instructed her to look at the date, which was for the next day. I told her having a small-town paper was key. Sam had printed tomorrow's front-page headline with the date in advance. I explained my plan was for her to travel over the next week and take pictures of local places like she had done before, but this time I would supply the newspaper with Alexandria's smiling face holding up our local paper with the current date on it. Everyone will think Alexandria was on vacation with Beth.

Beth asked, "How can you do that?"

"Our local newspaper will print the copies with advanced dates to look like a current edition. You'll email photos of you and local landmarks you want added. Make up some stories about where you are and what you're doing. Do whatever you want. Go wherever you feel like. Wherever the public thinks Alexandria might be is where the hordes will go. Make sure you stay one step ahead of them. It will appear that you have a newspaper reporter following you around."

She sat back for a minute and finally asked, "Do you think it will work?"

I said, "You did it before. You'll know the whole story in the next hour when our real local paper comes out. You only have a week or so before this is all over so why not try. You've got nothing to lose and everything to gain."

She asked, "What's in it for you?"

I replied, "Our little town will have a few days of peace and quiet before next week happens."

I told her Jeremy knows what's happening. "Go ahead, call him. See what he thinks."

She called Jeremy and after a few minutes she hung up. "We're in."

"Good. Here's my email address. Be sure to send the pictures and storyline you want forwarded to the editor no later than noon. The story will run the next day. We need one for Thursday, Saturday, and Monday." Alexandria's smiling picture and the date will be front-page news each day. The rest of the story will be concocted by Beth and Jeremy. "Just make it believable and stay ahead of the crowds," I said before she left my office.

Our local newspaper usually prints two thousand copies each day. On Tuesday it printed four thousand and delivered them like any other day at 10:00 A.M. to the local drop boxes. The lead story covered Alexandria's case and included a large photo of her on the front page. There were a lot of papers running stories about her, but ours had the scoop about the emancipation request. Sam had even gotten Jeremy to do an interview about everything. Of course, Jeremy's only concern was Alex's safe return. My name was mentioned as Alexandria's attorney. My life as I knew it was officially over.

By 10:30 Tuesday, my office was full of reporters and fortune hunters trying to be the first to locate Alexandria. I guess they thought I would hand out cards giving her whereabouts. I made a general statement about the case and the fact that Alexandria was living in a safe place waiting for her day in court. I also put out a statement from Alexandria that she had not been mistreated in any way by Jeremy or anyone else. She thanks her followers and hopes they will all understand this is about her and her future.

None of them were happy with the little bit of information I doled out. The national papers picked up our local news about the court case and the whole thing had gone international by the four o'clock news. News anchors speculated on why she wanted to be emancipated. Some went through the legal definition of emancipation. There were so many angles, the stories would be plentiful.

That afternoon, my assistant, Brenda, took her shopping list to the farmer's market. Being a woman, she gave it to one of the ladies who read it and filled it as normal. The camera and three special predated newspapers were inside her bag. I also added a note letting Alexandria know the judge had ordered an evaluation to make sure she was okay and understood what she was doing. I warned her early in the process that a mental evaluation might be requested. The last thing Brenda did was order a fruit basket to be delivered to Sam at the newspaper. Everyone understood what they needed to do.

I let Sam know to expect the fruit basket and he alerted me when it arrived. He called me when things were ready. A small crowd followed me to the newspaper where I bought what looked to be three copies of the daily newspaper. Although they looked normal, these were the special advanced copies of Thursday, Saturday and Monday's front page with a picture of Alexandria holding them and showing the date. My hope was by Thursday night a lot of the crowd would leave town and hunt elsewhere for the starlet. When I returned to my office, I inspected the advanced headline copies and emailed Sam that everything looked good.

A few hours later I received my first email from Beth with pictures. It appears she and Alexandria are staying close to Myrtle beach. They had taken some tours around Elizabethtown, North Carolina, then headed south for the beach. Beth included pictures of a couple of local restaurants and a picture of an expensive-looking hotel. There were also pictures of herself as well as photos of Alex standing and swimming at a beach. Jeremy must have had unpublished photos. It really did look like the girls were in South Carolina relaxing at the beach. I emailed the text and images to Sam at the newspaper so they could be inserted into the Thursday morning front page. Not everyone would leave town, but hopefully, it would be enough to give us a little breathing room.

After being followed home and seeing several spectators spending the night in their cars across the street, I turned off my lights and went to bed, fully aware that if I went downstairs for a glass of water someone would be watching. No matter what I said, I expected to be watched 24/7 from now on. I still had to figure out how Alexandria would be interviewed by someone for the judge.

At 9:00 A.M. on Thursday, the newspaper sent out its drivers and started filling up the racks with that day's news. On the front page was a smiling Alexandria holding our local paper with yesterday's date on it, making it appear that she was in South Carolina on Wednesday. The article said, "According to a local source in South Carolina, the internet star Alexandria Andres and friend Beth Carson were seen around their area on Wednesday." To protect his reputation as a professional journalist, Sam added a disclaimer at the end stating, "Members of this staff have been unable to verify this information sent by an anonymous source." It was the first time a photograph had appeared of the star in months.

The article didn't say a whole lot. Just showed the pictures and noted how great it is this time of year in South Carolina. The photographs showed a few local places to indicate where they were. It worked like a charm. I literally stood at the window and watched dozens of news reporters and thrill seekers hastily grab their equipment and head out of town. The chase was on.

Of course, not everyone left town, because the court date was less than a week away. But enough left to allow the citizens and merchants a chance to catch their breath and restock shelves. My tails stuck around and continued following my every move. Every day Brenda received over a hundred requests for interviews, including the big networks and major talk shows. None were granted. My ten days of fame were being spent hiding in plain sight. *The guy who wouldn't talk.*

The harassment got so bad, I had to call for a police escort to have a lunch at the diner and then I had to pick up their tab as well. It became a competition at the station as to whom would be my escort. Two or three officers sometimes showed up when I requested only one, forcing me to pay for everyone. My first intention was to tell the additional officers to leave then realized their meals could be billed as security. It was fun to watch a reporter come into the restaurant to ask for an interview and find a couple of officers sitting with me. They took great joy in asking reporters if it looked like I wanted to be interviewed at that moment. In their commanding way the officers answered for me, saying, "Call his office, if you want to set up an interview." Most of the reporters responded, "His secretary won't call us back." Causing the officers to shrug their shoulders and motion for them to move along. The tables next to us were always the quietest, because they were too busy listening to every word we said just in case I accidentally blurted out Alexandria's location, which never happened.

When the Friday paper came out the front page had a new photo of Alexandria holding up the local paper with Thursday's date on it. Same type of reporting as before. Locals had supposedly spotted the pair in Atlantic City, New Jersey. Lots of colorful pictures with Beth and supposedly Alexandria. I was shocked when I saw a photo of the two from behind, walking and carrying shopping bags. Apparently, Jeremy had hired a body double that was the same size and hair as Alexandria. The pictures shot from behind would have fooled me if I didn't know better.

The voice in my head screamed again, trying to convince me that it was her and everything was a huge publicity stunt. That deep fear of not knowing what to think had me in its clutches. I had no way of confirming where Alexandria was right now. I had no way of contacting her. *Calm down* I told myself, *she would not do this.*

I looked at the last photo and it had a frontal image of the pair. Beth's face was clear, but Alexandria's head was turned and covered by a hat flopping over her face. If it really was her why not show her face. I reassured myself the photos were part of my grand plan and nothing more, but the anxiety didn't go away.

EIGHTEEN

Alexandria was much better at playing this game than I ever could be. That realization hit me when a call came from the judge regarding her mental evaluation. He requested an emergency video session between me, Jeremy and his lawyer. Brenda set it up for 3:00 P.M. that day. When the call came in and all parties were present, Judge Richards informed us that Alexandria had met with someone about why she wants to be emancipated. They had a lengthy conversation. He decided to do this video session to speed things up and not have to deal with this portion next week. The judge stated, "It is my opinion that Alexandria Andres is of sound mind and completely capable of making her own decisions in regard to this court case. No further interviews with her are needed for this case to continue."

Jeremy asked, "Who interviewed her and when? We assumed we could be present and talk with her."

"I've made my ruling. You wanted her evaluated; it has been done. I saw no reason why you needed to be present. My clerk will email the ruling to you and we'll see you all next Wednesday." The call ended.

I sat back for a minute and thought. How did this happen? Who conducted the interview? I told Alexandria it needed to happen but how did she manage it? Who did she know that the judge would have trusted to do the interview? I emailed the judge's assistant and asked for a meeting. It came back immediately that he would meet me in his chambers at 4:30 P.M.

I went to the courthouse one hour later. At least two people tailed me. I almost admire their persistence and ability to keep following. Of course, a chance for the reward money was likely enough to maintain their vigilance. Since the local paper had scooped all the other news outlets on the upcoming case, the courthouse was slammed with requests for transcripts, keeping the clerks busy making and mailing copies. At least the paper salesman would see a boost in commission.

I was signaled into Judge Richards' chambers and sat down. The judge entered thirty seconds later. He started by offering me a piece of fruit from a fruit basket. I refused. Those fruit baskets had been flying around between me and the newspaper office for at least three days.

He started out by saying that since this is not a criminal case, he was not breaking the *ex parte* court rules prohibiting him from talking to me outside of court or opposing council. Plus, I already knew everything from Alexandria so we would not be discussing new information. He raised his water bottle and said, "I got to say, I'm not sure how this girl came to you, but you really have a once in a lifetime case on your hands. This girl is so smart and has nerves of steel. Imagine my surprise when I realized she's been hiding right in front of hundreds of people trying to find her. This morning someone knocked on my door. I opened it to see a girl holding this fruit basket." He nodded toward the large basket filled with summer fruit. "No one sends me gifts because they could be construed as bribes. I started to reject it, but the girl handed me the little card from the basket. Imagine my surprise when I read, 'I hear you want to talk to me. I am available now if you are. Signed Alexandria Andres.'"

I raised both hands and said, "I didn't know about any of this. I told her you wanted an evaluation. I never asked her to come and see you. "

The judge sat back and smiled. "To be honest I would have never thought of interviewing her myself. She told me her story in about thirty minutes. She is on top of the world right now. Fame and fortune. She could ride this gravy train for years. This is the kind of life most people would give their right leg for, abandoning their entire family in a heartbeat to be her. Instead, she wants to give it all up for a family. The only thing they offer is love and the kind of life that involves a lot of hard work that will never end. She is quite an amazing girl."

I realized what Alexandria had done. She had impressed the judge so much that she had won him over. The judge originally had questioned why she was petitioning the court now when she would be an adult in sixteen months. It now seems like sending her back to Jeremy would be the same as separating a family.

Sitting forward in his chair, the judge looked at me and said, "Bring me a sound argument as to her wanting to be emancipated. Show me she can take care of herself. This bunch from New York won't just release her. I understand why she wants to keep her new living situation a secret. Let's try to make that happen." Leaning back again, he smiled. "Before she left, I kidded her by saying, 'I thought you were in Buffalo, New York, or someplace like that?' As she left the room, she looked back over her shoulder and said, 'Check Monday's paper.'"

All I could do was say, "The sad part is I really don't know who she is staying with. I have no address for her. No real way to contact her. All I know is the family she is part of now has a great big guy that I would not want to tangle with. See you next week. Enjoy the fruit."

I returned to my office, with escorts tagging along, and fired up my laptop. I emailed Beth and requested that she be in Buffalo on Monday. I thought since Alexandria had hinted at it to the judge, we might as well make it happen. Going through my mail, I saw Brenda had picked up Alexandria's mail from her post office box. There was a letter from the GED company that likely contained results of her exam. I went back and forth about opening it and finally gave in, justifying my actions with needing the information for Wednesday's hearing and not sure when I would see her next. I used my letter opener to cut it open and slid it out of the envelope. It was addressed to her and read. "We are pleased to inform you that you have passed the exam and are now qualified to claim your GED certificate from the state offices. Please make sure to request your certificate within ninety days. Please send these results and $59 to the following address." I wasn't worried but it was one more thing off the list of things to do for the case. I marked it, "Please copy and send" and left it on Brenda's desk.

My email pinged. Beth informed me they would not be in Buffalo on Monday. They were in Chicago now and planned to be in Cincinnati on Monday. At least I knew what tomorrow's headline would be. As I sat there, I remembered that I had given them *carte blanche* to do anything they wanted, and they were taking full advantage. I decided to open Alexandria's page and see what Jeremy and Beth had been up to. When the page loaded, I was told my membership had lapsed. I had not been on the page lately, so I got out my credit card and found the subscription had increased by $5 and was now $24.99 for a one-month membership. The cost had gone up and Alexandria wasn't even there. I stared in amazement when I saw twenty-five hundred people were signed on to the website at that moment. I went to the newest videos and saw the titles, "Alexandria and Beth visit Myrtle Beach" and "Alexandria and Beth visit Atlantic City." The newest one about being in Chicago was not up yet.

I didn't take the time to watch them as I knew they were fake anyway. A button flashed that said, "Do you want us to come to your town?" I pushed it. It went to a page claiming the girls next stop would be at the city sending in the most money. People from all over the country and some abroad were encouraging others in the area to send money so Alexandria and Beth would visit their city, even though there was no guarantee that any town would be selected as their next stop. Jeremy and company were just getting free money—a big scam. A treasure hunt, where the prize stays two steps ahead of hopeful winners.

I was frustrated with the pair but what could I do? Then it hit me. They are not in charge. I can stop this at any point or at least change where they go. They had already bilked money from cities they they had no intention of visiting. I emailed Beth with the following note,

> *Beth: I'm sorry to hear you will not be in Buffalo on Monday. Alexandria has a press briefing scheduled at 2:00 P.M. to speak to all her fans about what is going on. This will be her first public appearance since she left. I'll inform her that you won't be able to attend. Regards.*

I closed my laptop and went home, practically guaranteeing to have emails from Beth waiting in my inbox tomorrow morning. I had deliberately not given her the name or address of the hotel nor did I plan to check my email before Monday morning. I was willing to bet money that Beth would be in Buffalo on Monday. When she and Jeremy show up and

Alexandria isn't there, they'll be furious, but what can they do, sue me? A thought passed through my brain. *Don't bookies take bets on anything?* I could get action on where Beth would be on Monday. If I didn't use Alexandria's name, the bet would pay off. *Who am I kidding?* I don't have a clue who to call to place a bet anyways.

NINETEEN

Saturday morning I walked out to the front yard to retrieve my newspaper and saw a young man standing on my sidewalk. He was a familiar face from among the many reporters I had seen around town, particularly those who staked out my house and office. I was surprised when he yelled my name.

I looked up and made eye contact.

"Where is Alex? I just want to talk to her."

Without opening the newspaper, I looked at him and said, "I think she's in Cleveland."

He shook his head. "I don't think so. I am not going to run all over while the bait keeps moving. I'm staying close to the source. I think she is right here in town somewhere."

I don't know why, but I asked where he was from and who he was working for. This was the first time I had spoken to a reporter one on one.

He said he was a newspaper reporter from a small town called Olean in southern New York. He was sent like everyone else to get the scoop by his boss. Normally, he reported on local sports, mostly high school games and such. He said his name was Tyler and raised his hand in a small wave. I liked his honesty. He didn't give me some lame reason. No camera out. No microphone in his hands. In the short two minutes we stood there talking, the attention of a couple more lookouts had been aroused. Three people approached. Two had cameras in their hands and readied them to shoot. In five more minutes, there would be a crowd.

"Do you have a family?" I asked.

"A wife and two boys are back home."

"How long have you been away from them?"

"About five days, but it seems like an eternity," he admitted.

I realized not everyone caught up in all of this were crazy fans. Tyler isn't some investigative journalist. He's just the guy his local newspaper could spare. I admired the fact that he hadn't taken the bait like so many others.

I boldly asked him, "Tyler, are you an honest man just trying to make a living? Do people respect you?"

He looked sheepishly down at the ground and said, "I always try to be a good example for my boys and someone my wife can be proud she married. I'm active in our church and coach my son's little league team."

"I don't think you're like most of the people who are here hunting her down. I'm going to trust your integrity. Would you like to come around to my back porch and have some iced tea and talk a while?"

He nodded he would, so I walked him around to the side fence, opened the gate and let him in. The now forming crowd, who had been warned by the police to stay on the public sidewalk, started yelling different questions in my direction. All the now rolling cameras recorded was me waving at them as the gate closed.

I showed Tyler to the back porch and invited him to have a seat at my patio table. I could not remember when I last had a visitor at my home. I went inside and retrieved two glasses and a pitcher of iced tea I had made for myself. Glancing around the kitchen I hoped to find a snack for us, but I had nothing in my cabinets. Then I saw the fruit basket sitting on the counter. Adding it to the tray, I made my way out to the back porch.

Tyler was standing and looking out at my backyard. He helped me with the door and said, "Nice yard. It must take a lot of time to keep it up."

I nodded that it did. I sat down the tray and poured two glasses of tea. He sat down and took a long pull and said, "I hope that fruit is on the breakfast menu. I haven't eaten since last night"

I opened the yellow wrapping paper from around it and said, "Dig in." He took out a banana, peeled it and started eating.

Like Alexandria had done with Beth I tried to figure out if this man was worthy of the scoop of his lifetime. I had the power to change this man's life forever. Alexandria had trusted Beth and it backfired. Beth went into business with Jeremey and switched over to the dark side. Tyler was older and had a family. I believed he deserved a break. "Where are your camera and microphone?"

"We're a small newspaper and mainly cover high school sports, ladies' groups, and church events. The editor only sends us out with pen and a note pad. I'm lucky he let me bring a laptop on this assignment. There's only one other reporter besides me."

He seemed worthy of a gift that would change his life. At the same time, I hoped this would not ruin his life.

"Do you already know the players—Alexandria, Jeremy and Beth?"

He said he did.

"Break it down for me, so I know you're up to date."

"Alexandria and Alex have separate websites and lives. The fact that one person played both people made a weird dynamic among the fans. The business they had going was making a lot of money. Something has changed since Alex went to a girl's jail for being a bully to some restaurant workers. She was then charged with assault." He paused for a second. "I never figured out why they didn't hire actors to play the role of the person being bullied so Alex wouldn't have gotten in trouble with the law."

"I had not thought of that," I said, "but Alex going to weekend detainment was such a media frenzy that it boosted her followers."

Tyler agreed and continued. "She went before the same judge, Judge Thomas, whom I learned was your college roommate."

No one else had made that connection. *Does Tyler know everything?* I wondered. *Is our scheme about to be revealed?* "Go on."

"He sentenced her to three years in jail, but then made a deal involving a six month detention at a work camp with a possibility of getting out after four months. That was the last time anyone saw Alex. A picture of Alexandria with Beth at the testing center turned up almost three months later, but nothing since."

I interrupted him by pointing out that Alexandria and Beth were traveling right now.

He sat back and smiled. "We have seen and heard a lot from Beth but not from Alexandria. Now, Alexandria has petitioned to be emancipated. She wants to become a legal adult and take care of herself. In short, she wants to be rid of Jeremy's shows. Jeremy does not want to release his golden goose. Beth," he said, "is an add on. She had one photo with Alexandria and has held on to her coattails ever since. The Beth trip is totally false. Just a way to keep people guessing and going to the website. And finally, you're the attorney trying to make it happen for her. Did I get it right?"

I nodded in the affirmative. "There is a lot more to it, but you have the main parts right." I picked up the newspaper and pointed to the main headline. Asking him I said, "What about Cleveland?"

He shook his head side to side. "Smoke screens. All of them. Jeremy's $50,000 reward is still out there. If Alex was really with Beth the reward would be taken down."

He was right. Jeremy was still trying to find her so he could try to change her mind. I decided to give him a chance. I looked at him and asked, "If I give you a story, do you think you can handle the pressure that comes along with it? It will change your life forever. Is that really what you want?"

Tyler lowered his head and brought his hands together, he was silent for about a minute, then raised his head and said, "I need to call my wife. This includes my whole family." I stood up and walked inside the kitchen so he could have some privacy as he made his phone call.

After his phone call, I looked out and saw him kneel with hands together stretched upwards. I realized he was praying to God for guidance. He stayed that way for a few minutes, then got up and sat back in the chair. I knew he was the right guy to help with my plan. I slowly opened the door and walked out on the patio and sat down. I couldn't tell by the look on his face whether he was in or out. I wanted him in.

After about thirty seconds he spoke, "I was sent here by my employer to report on this story. So far, I've only been able to write the same things that everyone else already knows. The fact that you picked me over the other hundreds of reporters to speak to assures me I am in the right place at the right time. I can handle whatever you have in mind. But you need to know that I will not do anything illegal or immoral, or anything that will compromise me or my family in anyway."

"What if I told you there was a bad guy who was taking advantage of a lot of people? A guy who has no morals and makes a lot of money in very sleezy ways. If I could point you in the right direction and you could catch him red handed, would you help me take him down? Keep in mind, however, that most of his dealings are legal. I believe a huge outcry from the public could at least slow him down. It will not stop him entirely but will slow him down. The story would go national, and surely change the life of the one who exposes him."

"We are talking about Jeremy, right?" Tyler asked.

I nodded my head yes and let him continue.

"I went on the Alex site and tabbed by most of the videos they had posted. By their titles you can tell he's pandering to the pornographic crowd. The number of views they get must be generating thousands of dollars. I assume your client has gotten the short end of the stick?"

"Negative," I exclaimed. "The grandmother negotiated a ten percent royalty of all income associated with Alexandria in perpetuity. Jeremy never expected her to become an international superstar. He set up bank accounts and the money has been rolling in since her stardom blossomed and even more since her incarceration. I expect Jeremy has embezzled a bunch off the top, but Alexandria is not concerned about that. I can't stop him, but I think we can slow him down."

Tyler smiled. "How can I resist such a noble cause?"

I was reminded of how Alexandria had referred to me as her knight in shining armor. I filled Tyler in on how the scam was working with crowd control in our town. The local newspaper was simply reporting what Jeremy and Beth fed them as anonymous contributors. I explained, "I just wanted some of the people to relocate for the town's sake."

He understood and mentioned he had pitched a tent at a local park because all the area hotels were booked up. He finally found an Airbnb three days ago as the crowds thinned. He was glad to have a place to shower.

"Jeremy and Beth overplayed their hand by hiring a double for Alexandria and actively telling people that Alex and Beth were together. Since all their videos are marked for entertainment only, they may not be breaking the law. Just imagine if you could catch them red-handed with no Alexandria. Exposing the lie might just slow him down. Either way it will be a scoop every other reporter would love to have."

Tyler rubbed his chin and looked up like he was thinking it over and then a frown came across his face. "I would need to know their itinerary and no one has a clue where they will pop up next." He explained.

I smiled and told him I knew exactly when and where they would be on Monday. He looked doubtful, then I explained how I had set them up to be in Buffalo. I did not share why I wanted them in Buffalo since he would then think I knew where Alexandria was right now.

Tyler had one day to think about how to break this story. He also needed more manpower and equipment. I pictured him ambushing them with cameras rolling and seeing the double. My headline would be, "JEREMY, YOU'VE GOT SOME EXPLAINING TO DO." It was Tyler's story to write, the only thing I could do was guarantee Alexandria would not be with them. I got his email and told him I would send the name and address of the hotel and the time Jeremy thought Alex would be there.

"The rest is up to you," I said.

I told him I hoped this didn't ruin his career as a coach. Sometimes stardom will do that. Hopefully, trusting him was the right thing to do. I gave him the fruit basket and let him out the side gate and wished him well. I peeked through the front blinds and saw about five camera crews surrounding Tyler trying to get information. For now, he was their focus. He would have to give them the slip.

Although it was the weekend, I went into the office, escorts in tow, and checked my email. There were three from Beth regarding Buffalo. I responded that Alex would be at the Ramada by Wyndham Niagara Falls at 10:00 A.M. on Monday. I told her the press conference was scheduled for 2:00, although nothing would be announced until noon on Monday. I also explained she did not want to see either one of them before the press release.

As I sent the email, I knew Jeremy and Beth would be packing their bags within minutes to get to Buffalo. Here was their chance to reach her before the court date. In case Jeremy tried to confirm Alexandria's presence in Buffalo I called the hotel and made a reservation for their best suite under the name Ann Andres for Sunday night. I paid with my credit card to guarantee the room. I would be expensing it out anyways so why not get the best the hotel offered.

I emailed Tyler the same information letting him know where Jeremy and Beth would be on Monday morning. I also told him to take the suite under Ann Andres since it was already paid for. No use wasting a free room.

While at the office, I decided to catch up on my billing hours for Alexandria's case. I opened the spread sheet. I had billed over a hundred hours on her case since the beginning of the initial consultation. That was over $10,000 with expenses. My retainer was only $10,000. Usually, I would be sweating over receiving the balance, but I knew her account was likely growing every day. I entered today's one hour with Tyler and the $495 suite I booked in Buffalo. Initially, Alexandria and Mark had tested me on the $10,000 one-time fee. I was glad I had refused.

Everything was laid out for my presentation to the court. Besides the money in her accounts proving she could sustain herself. We also had the GED letter putting to rest her schooling needs and, of course, a report from her interview with the judge settling her mental capacity. I don't know what her housing accommodations are. I can only assume she is living on a farm with a farm house on it. Alexandria's number one priority is to keep her new family out of the spotlight. Since the judge had interviewed her, he had to know who she was living with or at least have an idea what kind of housing she was living in.

When Jeremy was granted custody by Alexandria's dying grandmother, they had a simple custody document recorded. It was the best thing that could have happened to Alexandria at the time. The alternative would have been foster care. As much as I disliked Jeremy, he had taken care of her. The case should be ruled on this week and I saw no reason Alexandria should not be emancipated. I should have a few wrap-up hours, but after that this case should be over for me. Except the hundreds of expected requests for interviews, of which I plan to deny all of them.

I knew the secrecy of Alexandria's living arrangements was her top priority. The last thing she wanted was her new family exposed to the media. I called the sheriff. We went over a plan to get her out of the courthouse. I arranged a police escort out of town. With a little luck she could fade away and lay low for a while. Only a few more days and it should be over.

With the internet's help I decided to do a little research into the

Amish way of life, so I could answer questions that may come up. In reading, I found a lot of facts that I was unaware of. The Amish were not church members until after they went through rumspringa. When their youth are sixteen years old, they are encouraged to go out into the modern world and experience all the world has to offer. During this time anything they do will not be held against them. There is no set time as to how long rumspringa lasts for each person. When the youth decide they want to return to their Amish community and dedicate their life to the Amish Church they are then baptized into the church and become members of that community as an adult. About ten percent of the youth never return to the Amish way of life following rumspringa. That means they lose one out of every ten children to the modern world. If the child does not return, their existence is no longer recognized by the church. If they try to have any contact with their family, they are shunned. No one talks to them or makes direct eye contact with them. They are completely cut off from everyone they grew up with.

Alexandria had not spoken to me about joining the church. At her age she should be going through rumspringa right now. She had experienced everything the modern world had to offer and was giving it all up just to live the Amish life. I wondered if anyone had ever given up the modern world to become Amish. I am sure there have been a few who fell in love with an outsider and the outsider followed them back to the Amish way of life for love. What a hard transition that would be. Alexandria was surely the exception.

TWENTY

Monday morning, I woke up wondering how Tyler would approach Jeremy and Beth. I called the hotel and asked for Ann Andres room and was immediately put through. I was shocked to hear a woman answer and almost hung up. "Is Tyler there?"

"Yes, but he's in the shower."

Alarm bells started going off about Tyler. I didn't really know him. Who was this woman? "This is Ronald Woods. Would you ask him to call me when he can."

"Oh, hello. I'm Tyler's wife, Megan. Thank you for your generosity. Once he got to the room, he called and asked me to join him. Our house is only two hours away, so I accepted. This suite has more room than an apartment we once rented."

"I hope the two of you enjoy the room and please have him call when he has time.

"No problem," she said and hung up.

About ten minutes later my phone rang. It was Tyler. I asked about his plan, and he said he really didn't have a concrete one yet because he had figured out what I had not. Since Jeremy and Beth expected to see Alexandria there wasn't any need to bring the body double with them. That means my idea of catching them in the act was down the drain. They'll just claim Alexandria was a no show. *Why didn't I figure that one out?* I asked him to keep me informed and wished him luck.

Later that day I saw photos credited to Tyler that were picked up by area TV stations, showing Jeremy and Beth heading into the Ramada Inn. No Alexandria. When questioned on her whereabouts they hinted about a news conference around 2:00 P.M. with expectations of Alexandria being present.

That started a frenzy of news reports about what they thought she was going to say. At 2:00 P.M. the Ramada Inn's multipurpose room was filled with reporters anticipating Alexandria's arrival. The manager of the hotel went up to the microphone and announced there would be a Zoom meeting on the screen. The screen went on and I was live. I read from my prepared statement, "I am the attorney for Alexandria Andres, and we are putting out this statement to attest that Alexandria has not spoken to or seen Jeremy since before her incarceration. Any portrayal of her on vacation with Beth has been false. Alexandria would like to thank all her fans for their continued devotion but asks you all to stop looking for her and please go home to your families." With the statement read, I closed the meeting and began imagining the crowd gasping at what they just heard while Jeremy and Beth stood there with hundreds of reporters wanting answers.

I texted Tyler reminding him if he didn't want to sleep in the park again, he better call the Airbnb right away. This news conference and lack of information would surely drive the hordes back to our little town again. His short text of "OK" let me know he understood. I then walked to the diner to warn them to order extra food on their next delivery. They were sarcastically thrilled.

Stopping by the vegetable stand I handed over a short note informing Alexandria that all was ready for Wednesday and she did not have to attend. At the stand one of the older women took my note, read it and handed it to a younger girl who also read it and took it towards the back, handing it to whom I now knew was Alexandria. I realized there were no men helping at the stand anymore and guessed they had other jobs that needed more attention than hanging out at a farmers market every day. Alexandria started to fill a bag with fruits and vegetables. I hoped she didn't go overboard again. Being single and given the fact I ate out most meals, I didn't really need much. I saw her acting like she was checking off things on the list as she wrote a note back to me. I was relieved when she only put four items in the bag. The list was thrown back in the bag and handed back to the younger girl as she whispered in her ear. The younger girl brought it up to the older woman and whispered in her ear. The older lady handed me the bag and said with the three fruit baskets the cost is $95. I saw Alexandria smiling as she turned away. I had NOT ordered any fruit baskets this time. With the line looking at me, I got out my wallet and handed over $100. The woman asked if I was going to pick these up or have them delivered? I asked if they could be delivered to my office. The woman nodded in the affirmative. She also asked for another $10 for delivery charge. I handed over another $10 and said, "Keep the change."

I felt gouged, but knew this would all be expensed out on Alexandria's bill. Then it hit me. She also knew that would happen. She was purposely running up the bill. It occurred to me the people with whom she was staying were taking on an extra expense as well as disrupting their whole lives by having her in their home. I was certain they wouldn't take any money from her. This was her way of funneling some of her money to help her new family. I was sure the older woman had it figured out, but since the men were all away all they would know was the total income at the end of the day.

Returning to my office, it became evident that I really needed to find some new clients and new business for next week. In two days, we would be in court and one way or the other Alexandria's case would be ruled on. As I sat there, I heard the door open and Brenda say, "Please make your way to the conference room." I was hopeful a new client was here to discuss some upcoming business they needed handled. With such a small office, Brenda knew I was waiting to learn about the visitor. She came to my door and said, "A client is here to see you."

I gathered my pad and pens and went in to find Alexandria and young Amish girl. Alexandria had guts coming in during the middle of the day. She smiled at me and said, "We're delivering your fruit baskets, so we don't have a lot of time." I nodded as she continued. "I want to be in court on Wednesday. I want to talk to Jeremy and thank him for all he has done for me and also try to convince him to not contest my emancipation."

I told her I didn't think it would be wise, but it was her choice. "The hearing is set for 10:00 A.M. but no one expects you to be there."

"I'm counting on it. Please set up a meeting with Jeremy at 9:15. I'll be there by 8:00 when they open the doors. I will see you there," she said as she stood up. Then she smiled and said, "We left the three baskets with your secretary. Usually, we get a tip for deliveries."

I retrieved my wallet from my pocket and handed the other girl a $20 tip.

I asked Brenda to please take one of the baskets home. The last thing I needed was more fruit at my house. The last one was given to Tyler. I took the other two to the diner. At this point they were cutting them up and selling them as fruit plates. Free fruit is the least I could do for the diner since I had helped create such mayhem in the town and to their business.

Except for five walk-ins requesting interviews and multiple phone calls for the same, all of which Brenda turned down, the rest of the afternoon was quiet. Brenda was my watchdog, my gatekeeper. You had to get by her to get to me. I really needed to give her a raise. Maybe a bonus when this was all over. Thankfully, two more days and we should be finished.

I arrived at the diner on Tuesday at 8:15 to once again find a packed house. I saw Tyler at a booth in the back waving at me. Since he was all alone, I headed that way. As I sat down the waitress nodded at me. I knew my order had just been placed.

"Well, how was Buffalo?" I asked Tyler.

He smiled and said, "Not as productive as I had hoped."

I nodded in agreement. Then I explained, "I really thought I was giving you a scoop. I wasn't trying to send you on a wild goose chase."

"It wasn't all wasted," he said. "Since I was the first to get photos of Jeremy and Beth in Buffalo talking about the 2:00 P.M. press conference, I was able to get the story back to my editor who immediately uploaded to the wire services, making a good profit for the newspaper."

I had not realized it worked that way. So being first on the scene was key.

Tyler looked at me with an odd expression and said, "I arrived back late yesterday afternoon."

Okay, I thought, *he came back yesterday afternoon.* So had a bunch of other reporters when they realized Jeremy and Beth were playing them.

Then he leaned forward and whispered, "I figured it out. I know where Alexandria is staying."

I gasped a little. I don't have a good poker face, but then I have no idea where she's staying. I tried to compose myself, but he could tell I was shaken.

He continued, "I decided to follow my instincts and stay close to the source." He pointed at me and said, "That's you. You followed your normal routine. Nothing out of the ordinary. Fruit and vegetable stand and back to the office, then back to the diner with those fruit baskets you ordered again. Then it hit me. Who would give away all those fruit baskets? If I had not seen you give one away at the diner before, it wouldn't have registered. Plus, you gave one to me. You might have given one to the diner but why multiple ones? And then I thought, maybe I should get myself some fresh fruit. So, I went to the stand and was helped by the older woman just like you and the order was packed by the girls in the back. After I was done, I walked around to the side and guess who I saw packing fruits and vegetables?"

There was no denying it. He had already read my face. He knew Alexandria was hiding in plain sight. My heart fell as I imagined the frenzy this would cause her and her new family. The gig was up. I asked, "When are you calling Jeremy to collect the bounty on her?"

He leaned forward and whispered, "I'm not." He continued, "I called my wife and explained the situation and we both realized while we could use the bounty money there was a good chance Jeremy would skip out on paying it. Plus, if you play in the pig pen you come out stinking like the pigs. I told you I wouldn't do anything unethical. This is borderline, but I'm not going to be the one to blow her cover."

Then he informed me that he was heading home tomorrow to be with his family. He was done with this story. He finished his meal and stood to leave, but not before leaning over to whisper in my ear, "Stay away from the fruit stand." He also slipped his breakfast ticket under my plate.

All he received for finding the golden ticket that the whole world was looking for was a free breakfast at the diner. As he walked away, I remembered seeing him bow his head on my porch, asking God for guidance. I had trusted him, and he had not let me down. I thought, *We need more men in this world like Tyler.*

I ate my breakfast and went back to my office. It felt like every set of eyes in town were following me as I walked down the street. Everyone was looking for Alex and she was only a block away.

TWENTY-ONE

Back at the office, I asked Brenda to get Jeremy on the phone for a conference call. She set up a time for 10:00 A.M. He was in town and wanted to come to the office. "We'll see him in court tomorrow. I just want to run something by him." Since he had been warned by the sheriff about coming to my office, he agreed.

At 10:00 A.M. Brenda called him back and conferenced me in on the call. Evidently, Jeremy had spoken to a few lawyers and had gotten opinions that he might lose the case. Alexandria could be granted emancipation.

He started out friendly like we were old buddies from a long time ago. "How are you?" he asked.

I said, "Fine," but left it at that.

He and I both knew I had set them up in Buffalo with Tyler and the fake press conference, but Jeremy also knew getting confrontational would only stir the pot. He wanted something and was trying the "get more flies with honey" approach.

I confirmed we would be in front of the judge at 10:00 A.M. Wednesday. He affirmed that time. "I have a few things to run by you before the hearing. Can you meet me at 9:15 in the courthouse conference room?"

He said he had time today, but I told him I was waiting on an important part of the case that wouldn't be available until 9:00 A.M. tomorrow. He agreed to the meeting. Then he surprised me.

"You know I really do care about Alexandria. We have worked together over three and a half years. She is like a daughter to me. I'm not really sure what is going on?"

I told him I would see him in the morning.

After I hung up the phone, I thought about it. Jeremy had cared for her and made her an internet star. Most teenagers would love to be in her shoes. All the money and fame you could want. Not to mention the power that comes with being an influencer. If she wears someone's clothing line on one of her shows, that designer sells out in less than a day. What more could a kid want.

Alexandria had grown up pretty much on her own since her grandmother had taken her in. Jeremy was as close to a father as she had ever known, but all he wanted from her was the money she generated. She had acknowledged that he took care of her needs and had done nothing wrong. For the first time in her life, Alexandria had not only found one person to love her but a whole family. The hardship and burden she was creating for this new family was huge. Although my childhood was good, I never felt the love she was experiencing right now. People she didn't know four months ago were willing to risk their way of life for her. That's total, unconditional *agape* love. She had found it and never wanted to let it go.

Knowing Alexandria would be at the courthouse at 8:00 A.M., I decided to meet up with her at 8:15. I would be followed and didn't want to arrive too soon and risk being seen with her.

As I went in, I saw two girls delivering fruit baskets so I approached them, asking if their baskets were for sale? It was hard to tell but the older girl was probably close to Alexandria's age and the other one was very young. They both looked at the floor and the young one hid behind the older sister's leg. The older girl very quietly said, "No."

I didn't want to attract any unwanted attention, but I needed information from them, so I retrieved my wallet and quietly said, "I am Alexandria's attorney. I am trying to get her free so she can come and live with you folks. She told me about her new family." The little one peeked her head around and I continued, "I believe you would be Hanna." With that, the little girl quickly retreated behind her sister's leg.

Hearing Hanna's name, the older girl knew I was legit. "I am here to meet with her but I don't know where she is."

As I pulled out money for the basket of fruit the older one said, "Room nine at the end. The baskets are $70." I did not need two more fruit baskets but what was I going to do. I handed her $70. And as she handed me the baskets, she made eye contact and added, "Plus tip." She had learned from Alexandria. I pulled out another $20 and handed it to her. As I walked away, I heard her say, "Enjoy the fruit." I stopped for a second and then just lowered my head and smiled. I headed for conference room nine.

Outside room nine, I stopped for a second and made sure no one was following me inside the courthouse. I quietly knocked and slowly opened the door. Alexandria sat at the opposite side of the conference table. She stood and offered her hand. I stepped up and shook it as I looked her up and down. She was dressed in loose fitting jeans and a tee shirt that said, "I love puppies." Not exactly what I would wear to court but I am not a teenage internet star. Her long hair was pulled back into a ponytail that hung down her back. She wore no makeup or jewelry. Her face had a great tan and she looked well-toned and healthy. Today would be the world's first look at her since she disappeared.

She didn't look down or act demure. She looked right into my eyes, reading my thoughts. She began by saying how happy she was to see me. Then she asked if anything was wrong. I told her I just thought we could spend a few minutes together and go over any questions she may have. She assured me that she was ready for whatever came.

Since she didn't have any questions, I sat across from her. A few seconds passed and she started to smile at me. "What's so funny?" I asked and she pointed at the two fruit baskets I had placed on table. I smiled back and said, "Those two baskets cost $70 plus tip. Before meeting you I never carried that much cash. I have learned I better carry some with me." Then I told her, "You know I am writing these off as an expense against your account, right?"

She nodded and asked, "Did you get a receipt for those? If you paid cash and didn't get a receipt, they cannot be reimbursed." I started to raise my hand in protest as I thought of how many baskets I purchased and didn't have a receipt for any of them. Then I looked at her face, she was smiling at me.

"I guess I can let it slide this time," she said.

After a few more seconds, I asked out of curiosity, "Why the 'I love puppies' on your shirt?"

She explained, "When you are being watched by potentially millions of people you must think about everything you say and wear. If you wear a certain type of jeans you are endorsing them. If your shirt says 'I love New York,' then everyone in New York is happy but the rest of world could be offended because you didn't say you liked their city. Unless you are trying to promote something or someone you must stay neutral. Who in the world could get upset that I love puppies? That's how the show made a lot of its money. Through sponsorships. When we went to the beach parties, we were always in a Jeep product. They provided those trucks and paid us to use them. Jeremy really knows how to work the system. Everything is legal but sometimes the sponsors are not the most reputable people. Especially on the Alex side."

I sat there for a moment thinking how hard it must be just to make sure you weren't wearing something that would offend anyone, let alone have every word you spoke being a potential *faux pas*. The pressure to keep it all straight must be enormous. I looked down at the outdated suit and tie I had on and realized I am good material for a comedy sketch. The people she lives with all dress exactly the same. That really removes the pressure from a lot of things. No more individuality. Just clothes. No trying to keep up with the Jones.

"Are you sure you want to completely cut off the outside world? I did some research and know you can't be half in and half out. Is there anyone you want to stay in contact with?"

She shook her head from side to side. "I have no living relatives," she said. "Everyone I know is connected with the show, either through acting alongside me or behind the scenes. Jeremy cares for me but doesn't love me. No one does. There were many nights when I was left all alone in my side of the house. No one to talk to or share things with. I now have that, and, yes, that is why giving up everything else isn't a problem."

I asked if she knew about rumspringa and she said, "Yes, I am the reverse of that. No one in our community has ever known this to happen. When a young adult decides to go on rumspringa the parents know this might be the last time they ever see their child. The ones who leave the community are shunned and not spoken to ever again. I experienced it for a while, and it was no fun. Some just simply disappear and are never heard from again. Can you imagine never knowing what became of your child?" She continued, "There is one particular day when the rules are not enforced, but no one speaks of it." She looked at me and asked, "Do you know the diner about six miles out of town?"

I nodded my head yes. I knew where it was. Just an old highway diner out in the middle of nowhere.

She explained, "Once a year on that child's birthday the parents go to that diner for a couple of hours and are allowed to visit with their shunned children. Some of the shunned come just to catch up or to introduce children to their grandparents. Some mothers have gone to that diner for years hoping their child will finally show up. Some never do. The young adults are welcome to come back and reassert their faith anytime and be accepted back into the community—if they are willing to give up the outside world. The longest one I heard about returned after twenty-two years in the outside world. So, there is always hope in the parents' minds. Some children never make contact and never even know when their parents pass away. It is so heartbreaking on the mothers.

"That is why my giving up the outside world is so unusual. There have been a few who went out and found a mate and brought them back to the community, but it's a rare occurrence. I am the first to just want to stay. I have not asserted to follow the church one hundred percent but the fact that the family has accepted me as one of their own gives me time to decide what I'm going to do. My story is so well known in our community that they have reached out to other Amish communities for church guidance on my situation."

I stopped her there and asked, "Are you telling me a hundred plus people know who you are and where you are living and no one turned you in for the $50,000 reward?"

She smiled and continued. "There are probably thousands of Amish who know who I am and approximately where I am staying. I am a unicorn to them. I represent all the ones who never find their way back. If someone reported me and received the reward, they would be shunned and never allowed back into the church. In their world they are dead to everyone else."

I then thought back about Tyler's decision not to blow Alexandra's cover. *To some people honor is worth more than money.*

I reminded her if the judge did not grant her emancipation, she would legally have to return to Jeremy's custody or be considered a runaway.

She nodded in agreement. Then stated, "In sixteen months I will be eighteen years old and will return as an adult no matter what. I have a family now and responsibilities that I must uphold." She asked me, "Do you know that the oldest daughter is responsible for the youngest daughter? Hanna is mine to look after. Mine to mentor and teach. The family has given me a great honor in trusting me to do that job. I will not let them down. No one has ever had that much faith in me. If I must go back to Jeremy's custody, I cannot contact them for fear of exposing them to reporters and the whole world. That is their biggest fear, but they risk it each day I am with them. The thought of losing sixteen months is unbearable. The sad part is we cannot tell anyone where I live. I just hope the judge will be able to understand and make the right ruling."

The fact that Alexandria could be taken away and forced to live with Jeremy is a possibility, but hopefully not a reality. I explained, "Your conversation with the judge and laying out your story, getting him on our side, has eliminated many variables. Although the judge doesn't know where you're staying, he is convinced it's a clean and safe environment. During the court hearing Jeremy will probably try to assert that he is your best option for the next sixteen months. He hopes to convince you in those months to reengage with your audience once again."

She sat up defiantly and said, "I am not that person anymore. I will never play his characters ever again."

To that fact I had no doubt.

"How do you want the meeting with Jeremy to playout?"

"Just Jeremy and his attorney, you and me in the room. I want to take this head on," she answered.

TWENTY-TWO

Jeremy and his attorney stood at the end of the hall along with several other people, including Beth. I asked him if we could have a couple of minutes for a brief discussion. Our conversation aroused the interest of reporters milling around the hallway. The whole group started to head back with us when I turned and said, "The room is small just Jeremy and his attorney, please." They all sighed at being dismissed but the argument of the small room seemed valid. Little did they know Alexandria was only ten feet away. I opened the door slowly, noticing that Alexandria was not visible and let Jeremy and his attorney in. I quickly entered behind them and closed the door.

I watched as Jeremy turned to sit down and made eye contact with Alexandria. He was shocked at first, then composed himself. He had been trying to get an audience with her forever and here she was. I'm sure he had played out what he was going to say to her a thousand times in his head. Here was his chance.

He started off in the worst possible way. "Alex, we've been so worried about you."

The fury in Alexandria's eyes was unmistakable. I learned from our first encounter that she NEVER wanted to be called Alex. That persona represented the worst of the worst in humankind in her opinion. To Alexandria's credit I saw her shoulders drop and the rage disappear. After all, how would Jeremy know this. The last time they had spoken, the two were conspiring how to make the most of her jailtime antics.

She politely responded, "I am good. By the way I only go by Alexandria now."

You could tell by the way Jeremy was fidgeting that he wanted to just blurt out all the arguments swirling in his mind.

Alexandria took the lead by saying, "First of all, Jeremy, I want to thank you for all you have done for me. I have no idea where I would be right now if not for you. I understand you are confused as to what has happened. In short, I have discovered there are good people out there who simply work hard and try to live an honorable, meaningful life. Until a few months ago, my life was all about money and fame. I have no family to love me and no one who really cares about me. You made sure my needs were met, but in the end I'm all alone. I do not want that life anymore. The one I have now is something you cannot provide."

Taken aback, he processed what she said then his smile suddenly appeared. He said, "Hang on a minute. I may have a solution." He went outside for a minute, then re-entered the room with a woman. The woman was blond and had on plenty of makeup. She wore tight-fitting shirt and nice dress slacks. I couldn't place her but thought I knew her.

Evidently, Jeremy had warned her because she extended her hand and said, "It's nice to see you, Alexandria."

Alexandria extended her hand and said, "It's nice to see you, Ann." Alexandria looked at me and explained, "Ann plays my mom on the series."

Then I realized she appeared in some of the videos. Although it was only weeks ago it seemed like years. So much had happened since then. She was the one who did the house tour video and workout videos that were advertised. Although she was not the main character, she probably had a big following herself. I wondered if her agent had been smart enough to negotiate ten percent of the total proceeds from all the shows?

Ann started by saying, "I know you've been through a lot and want a change in your life. My husband and I want to become your legal guardians. You would live with us and become our family. We don't have any other kids, but Beth has agreed to move in with us also. You two are already friends, so we thought it would be great to have her around. What do you think?"

Alexandria calmly stated, "Thank you for the offer, but I want to reiterate what I told Jeremy, I will NEVER be a part of the home series again. That part of my life is over. All you are offering is a change of address. I want to oversee my own life. I no longer want the money or the fame."

Ann looked at Jeremy and said, "It's not happening, she wants out, and there is nothing I can say to change her mind." She walked over to Alexandria, gave her a hug and whispered in her ear. "Good luck, sweetie. I hope you find what you're looking for." After that Ann walked around the table and exited out the door.

Jeremy was sure Ann was his ace in the hole, but she was shot down. He stared at Alexandria for about thirty seconds trying to figure out what to say. Then I announced, "Gentlemen, we will see you in the courtroom." I motioned toward the door, and they accepted defeat in this round and walked out.

Alexandria shed a few tears after what Ann had said and then she came over to me and put her arms around me and gave me a quick hug. Stepping back, she said, "You have been my champion all this time. No matter what happens, I want you to know I appreciate your willingness to turn your life upside down to help me"

I looked at her and said, "I want to thank you also for mixing up the humdrum life I was living. But I also want to remind you that you tricked me. I agreed to all this before I even knew what was going to happen." With that said we both broke out in smiles.

I asked her what our next move would be? She said, "A press conference to announce to all my fans that I am leaving the show."

We both knew there was plenty of press in the building but we still had an hour before the court time. I asked her to give me a minute. I called Tyler. "Where are you?" I asked.

"I'm just loading stuff in my car to leave, why?"

"Get over to the courthouse, conference room nine and bring your camera, quickly," I directed.

"Okay, be there in five minutes," he responded.

I turned back to Alexandria and said, "In a couple of minutes, I am going to send in the one reporter in the world I trust. His name is Tyler. He is from a small newspaper in southern New York State. He came to me when he figured out where you were and did not tell anyone. I know he is an honorable man. I believe you and he will get along nicely and work well together. It is up to you whether you want a yelling screaming mob or a one-on-one interview where you control what is said."

Her response was, "Please send him in when he arrives."

In a couple of minutes, I went out to the main corridor and was besieged by more than fifty reporters and cameramen. All were shouting and yelling at me about Alexandria now that they were aware she was in the conference room. It was a mad house. I made my way to the front doors and saw Tyler trying to push through but was having no luck. I started to yell, and everyone got quiet. "Attention everyone. Alexandria will do a live interview in a few minutes. Please clear the building and proceed to the front steps."

Hearing this they all scampered out to set up for the big shot. As Sam, our local newspaper editor, came out of the courtroom, I grabbed him by the arm and spun him around. He tried to pull free then looked me in the face and said, "I am going outside."

I pulled him near and said, "I think you should use the facilities before you leave. And make sure you wash up after you are done."

His eyebrows went up as he scanned my face. "I think I will."

I asked the security guard if he could find a podium we could use outside. He was so happy the building was cleared that he smiled and immediately searched for one. Even the spectators in the courtroom made their way to the front steps. No one wanted to miss the big press conference. Jeremy, Ann, Beth and their attorney stood to the side at the top of the stairs where they could quickly slip in and become part of the news conference.

I waved at Tyler to come forward and whispered in his ear. He went inside. Although the other reporters saw him enter the courthouse, they weren't about to give up their vantage point for the press conference. As the podium was brought out, I went back inside and saw Tyler standing next to conference room nine. The news reporters were ready for live coverage as all the networks had announced they had breaking news about Alexandria. As they stood there waiting for the internet star to emerge, I wondered how many times they would tell their viewers to hold on for a few more seconds. I didn't say there would be an interview with them, I just directed them to the steps. They assumed it would be outside. By the time they got restless, Tyler was all set up in the room ready to start the interview. After a quick introduction of Alexandria to Tyler, they were off.

It seemed fitting that Tyler get the scoop since he could have blown her cover but chose not to. He started by thanking Alexandria for the interview. I heard her say how appreciative she was of all her fans and thanked them for their friendship and love. At that point I quietly closed the door and left them to do their thing.

Twenty-Three

The crowd outside the courthouse grew larger and louder. I stepped up to the podium, everyone got quite when I raised my hand. I was trying figure out what to say, when someone yelled, "How much longer?" That gave me an inspiration and told the crowd, "Please give us about five more minutes. We're trying to find some kind of sound system we can use." With that said, I re-entered the building, stopped and asked the security guard to call the sheriff for back up. From there, I quickly went to the court clerk's office and asked to speak to the judge. Aware of the situation, he saw me immediately. I asked him for a favor. He granted it. Ten minutes later, I was back outside.

A portable sound system was set up on the podium. Three sheriff's deputies had arrived. I waved them up the steps to the front door, and handed the courthouse security guard an order just signed by the judge. I ushered him towards the podium and microphone, he scanned the paper and looked back at me, shaking his head. With all the live cameras pointed at him, and everyone quiet. They heard him say, "Not happening. This is way above my paygrade." He handed the paper back to me and went back inside the building.

With no other choice, I went to the podium and announced, "We all know the courthouse is publicly accessible during normal business hours. You also know that proceedings inside the courtroom cannot be recorded by either video or audio. Only handwritten reporting is allowed inside the courtroom. Because today is highly irregular, the judge has issued an order stating that due to safety concerns all lobbies, corridors and foyers are closed to the public for today only. No one is allowed to enter the courthouse who is not directly part of the upcoming case. In other words, if you're not in the building now you're not coming in."

I turned and retreated towards the door. The faces on the sheriff's deputies were priceless. On national television I had just announced to the world they would not get any coverage from the courtroom.

A reporter yelled out, "You said there was going to be an interview with Alex."

I smiled and turned back around and when they all got quiet, I said, "Alexandria is doing an interview right now in conference room nine. I never said it would be out here or that you were invited. I suggest you contact the Olean newspaper in southern New York if you want a copy of the interview. The crowd erupted in total chaos.

Leaving the deputies to handle crowd control, I retreated inside and made my way to conference room nine. The two were still talking. Tyler's cell phone vibrated. I told him he had better just shut off his phone for a while. He looked at the number then sent it to voicemail. It immediately vibrated again. This time he shut it off. I told him, "You are going to be very popular."

As I listened to the interview it was evident Tyler already knew that Alexandria was staying with an Amish family, and did not push her on the location. He understood that piece of information was to remain confidential. It was a perfect fit for the two. She was telling her fans goodbye and asking them to respect her privacy. A controlled, respectful interview. I was glad Tyler was the one doing it but I also knew this would change his life forever. Talk shows will want interviews with him. Personally, I wouldn't be doing any. It's his life, he can choose to or not.

The interview only lasted a few more minutes. I heard her thank Jeremy and Ann and all the other cast members. She wished them all happiness and joy in their lives and the interview was over. Tyler looked at her and said, "That was a great way to end your story. Now hopefully you can get the closure you want and ride off into the sunset. I have read so much about you and your story I feel like I know you."

She gave him a small hug. "Thank you for letting me say what I wanted to say. Please stay honorable. We have brought a lot of fame and a lot of problems on you. It's going to be tough on you and your family."

He brought his hands together in a praying pose as he exited.

As soon as we were in the hallway, I told him how I had gotten the rest of the reporters banished from the courthouse. He smiled in disbelief. At that point Sam approached me and said, "Well, I guess I stayed too long in the restroom. I missed being banished." I introduced the two of them and Tyler commended Sam on his breaking of the courtroom story.

Sam winked at me and explained, "I was just in the right place at the right time." He looked at Tyler and pointed to the courtroom, and said, "After you." They both slowly headed towards the courtroom.

Tyler asked Sam, "Would you be interested in some photos I just got from my interview with Alexandria?"

I yelled at them, "You both owe me breakfast."

They both turned to face me as Tyler said, "Maybe we should send him something."

Sam chimed in with, "How about a nice fruit basket?" Chuckling, they turned and entered the courtroom.

I returned to conference room nine and Alexandria asked about the time. "We have about thirty minutes before we're due in court."

"Is Jeremy in the hallway?"

"No, he must already be in the courtroom."

"Good," she said, "Follow me." She led me ten feet down the hall to door number eight, knocked and entered, motioning me to follow.

Walking in, I was shocked to be surrounded by a whole room of Amish people. Alexandria with her head down went up to the biggest man in the room and said, "I would like to introduce you to my father, Jonathon."

The big man towered over me as he stretched out his huge hand that covered mine. I could feel how rough his hands were from all the years of hard labor. I looked into his now gentle eyes, but remembered the look he had given me at the fruit stand when he thought I was a threat to his family. He only said two words, "Thank you!"

I shook his hand and said, "You're welcome."

Looking at about ten people, I asked, "Who are all these people? She said, "My family."

"Which ones?"

She smiled and waved her hand all around and said, "All of them."

If she was looking for a family, she hit the jackpot, I thought. As I looked around the room my eyes fell on the youngest girl. She retreated behind Alexandria's leg hanging on tight. I did not want to alarm her, so I asked Alexandria, "Is this the legendary Hanna?" The girl got even smaller behind her big sister's legs.

Alexandria reached back to pat her on the head and said, "Yes, she is. The one and only."

I scanned the others and put them in chronological order. The mother. The older son and wife. A couple of other boys and three girls. There was an older gentleman that I stopped to look at. Although they all had similar clothing, his was a little different.

He saw me looking at him and said, "I am the Church Bishop. I lead the local congregation."

I reached out and shook his hand. "She has a lot of people looking out for her," I said.

The bishop nodded his agreement.

"Jonathon, how do you intend to get everyone out of here unseen?"

He pointed to the back of the room and said, "The same way we got in."

I looked toward the back and saw six fruit baskets lined up.

He explained, "We needed to be here today to support our daughter. Most people never pay much attention to us. Besides we plan to use the back alley when we leave."

I thought the plan was a little shaky, but it wasn't up to me to make sure their cover wasn't blown.

"Alexandria, I'll meet you in the courtroom. Take a few more minutes with your family." She smiled and I left them alone. I made eye contact with Hanna and waved at her, causing her to once again retreat into the safety of Alexandria's protection.

Inside the courtroom, Sam and Tyler sat next to each other on the far side. They were the only people in there at the time. I went to the center section so I would be close to my table once we were called up front. About thirty seconds later Jeremy and his attorney came in and sat a couple of rows behind me.

A minute later Jeremy spoke to me. "You know that little stunt you pulled made it tough. The cops didn't even want to let us in."

I could barely hide the smile that crossed my face.

He continued. "That crap would not happen in any other courtroom."

At that I turned to him and said, "Maybe you should express your feelings to the judge and make a motion that would overturn his order."

Jeremy looked directly at me. You could see his mind trying to come up with something to rebuff me with, but he had nothing. His eyes went blank, and he turned to his attorney and mumbled, "They are not the only ones with a surprise."

TWENTY-FOUR

What was Jeremy and his attorney planning? Everything was laid out to get her emancipated. Alexandria has the means to support herself; she has her GED; and the judge knows she has a safe place to live and understands why she wants a different life. The guardianship was a good thing for Alexandria but now she wants something different. I also planned on bringing up the fact that under Jeremy's watch Alex had been in trouble with the law twice. How fit is he to be her guardian? I had no clue what I was missing.

A few minutes before the hearing was to begin, Alexandria came in and sat beside me. Then the court bailiff and recorder entered. Precisely at ten o'clock the judge entered as the bailiff yelled, "All rise." Judge Anthony Richards waved at us to be seated. The bailiff then announced, "The case in front of us is a continuance of case number 8195764. The case involves Alexandria Andres, a minor living in the state of Pennsylvania who is seeking emancipation."

The judge asked if all parties were present and looked our way. I stood up and stated my name and pointed to Alexandria as the partitioner. The judge once again pointed to the left table. We proceeded past the partition to the table. He then looked at Jeremy and his attorney who stated their names and were directed towards the table on the right.

The judge continued. "This case is pretty straight forward. Miss Andres wants to be emancipated and take care of her own affairs and considered a legal adult. Previously, the court had ordered Miss Andres be

149

interviewed to evaluate her mental capacity and understanding of what she was trying to accomplish. The petitioner has been interviewed and found to be of sound mind and has explained herself as to why she wants to be emancipated. I am satisfied with her evaluation and her living conditions."

At that Jeremy's attorney raised his hand to be recognized. I knew what was coming. Jeremy's attorney was about to step in it. The judge motioned him to stand, and he said, "Your honor, we have not been given any type of formal report as to what was said and who she said it to. We do not even know if that person was qualified to evaluate her mental state."

Alexandria and I looked at each other. We were both grinning from ear to ear.

The judge looked at him and said, "I already gave my findings. If you must know, I personally had a one-hour, on-camera interview with Miss Andres and found her intelligent as she laid out compelling reasons for not wanting to be under her current guardian's care. There are no allegations that your client did anything wrong. In fact, she stated her appreciation of everything he has done for her. I am satisfied that she understands what she is doing. In fact, I will state that I find her to be mature beyond her years."

I whispered into Alexandria's ear. "An on-camera interview is where the judge personally investigates confidential or private matters before deciding if they should be made public. He has made the decision to keep your living arrangements out of the public record."

When the judge finished his remarks, Jeremy's attorney sat down. Alexandria knew she had won the judge over. I could not think of any objection Jeremy might have that would sway the judge in a different direction.

Over the next hour I laid out Alexandria's financial situation. She now had over $1.3 million in the bank. With her being gone the last four months, money had poured into her account.

I also showed her post office box rent to prove she was a resident of the state. Her GED was also submitted.

The last thing we did was put Alexandria on the stand. We figured the less she said the better. She simply stated that she wanted to start over in a new life without a public audience observing her every action. A quiet, simple, normal life.

After she made her statement, Tom Dugan began questioning her. "We don't understand how this could have happened so abruptly. Are you involved with a guy?"

She shook her head no.

"Miss Andres, you'll need to verbalize your response for the court reporter," the judge reminded her.

Her response was a simple "No."

She was asked about her living arrangements, at which point she looked at the judge.

Judge Richards addressed the attorney. "I have already told you that where she is living has been determined to be safe and satisfactory."

Dugan was running out of arguments and finally said, "I have no more questions for her."

I thought, *Is that it?* They had not objected to anything that would sway the judge. Then that little tingle feeling crept up the back of my neck. *Something is wrong.* I had no idea what, but recalled Jeremy mentioning a surprise.

As Alexandria sat down, Jeremy's attorney proclaimed, "Your Honor, we have one more interested party that we would like you to hear from."

The judge nodded his approval.

Jeremy's attorney said in a loud voice, "We would like to have Alan Johnson take the stand for a statement."

We turned to see a man dressed in an army uniform enter the courtroom and approach the witness stand. The judge asked the bailiff to swear him in.

Tom Dugan said, "Please state your name, military rank and the reason you are here."

"My name is Alan Johnson. I'm a master sergeant in the United States Army and I'm here today because I think I may be Alex's father."

I Looked at Alexandria and whispered, "Can this be true?"

She shrugged her shoulders and whispered back, "I have no idea. I never knew my father. My mother nor grandmother ever told me anything about him."

I looked over at Jeremy. Now, it was his turn to grin.

His attorney continued, "Why do you think you may be her father?"

Master Sergeant Johnson straightened up in his chair and stated, "When I was nineteen years old, I had a one-night stand with a girl from Alexandria's hometown the night before I shipped out for basic training. We met in a bar and hit it off. We had a great time. We laughed and talked for hours. Since the Iraq war was going strong in 2006 there was a good chance I would be deployed. One thing led to another that night and that's why I think I might be Alex's father."

Attorney Tom Dugan, asked, "Did you ever see this girl again?"

"No, I did not," Alan Johnson confessed. "After boot camp I was deployed to Iraq and never went back there. I swear I never knew we had a child together."

Attorney Dugan asked, "That's all well and good, Mr. Johnson, but what makes you think you are her father instead of someone else?"

Alan Johnson continued. "I read about Alex missing and the article mentioned that she never had a father. After realizing I was around at the right time, I called Jeremy to make sure the report was correct regarding there being no father. Jeremy told me he didn't know anything about her biological father. We met. I never knew the last name of the lady I had the encounter with. The only name I remember her giving me was her first name, Annie. I am not sure, but I think I may be Alex's father."

I felt Alexandria move and turned to watch her shrink into her chair. Her head was down, and her eyes were closed as if she was praying. I looked over at Jeremy and the grin on his face grew. There would have been a loud gasp in the courtroom except there were only a few of us in there at the time. My mind raced on what to do next. With all the choices I had in front of me I had to choose one. My hand shot up and the judge looked up at me and waved at me to speak, I blurted out, "May we have a brief recess, I would like to consult with my client?"

As the door closed to the conference room, I asked, "Alexandria, could his story be true?"

She looked at me with tears in her eyes. "I don't know. The only thing I am sure of is that my mother's name was Ann but she went by Annie. Ann Andres is the stage name for the women who played my mother on the show. When Jeremy started the shows my mother had passed away. My grandmother asked him to name my internet mom Ann to remember her by."

I reached out my hand in comfort and she took it. I looked into her eyes and said, "So Master Sergeant Alan Johnson could be your biological father? His story may be true."

She tightened her grip on my hand. "Yes."

We sat there for a few seconds, and I suddenly went into attorney mode. I let go of her hand and sat up in my chair. I took out a piece of paper and told her, "This could change everything. What do you want to do if he is your father? He could have parental rights."

I could tell this was messing with her head, but I also knew how smart she was. Her eyes glazed. She was trying to figure out the next step. I took charge. I looked her straight in the eyes and said, "I know this is a lot to comprehend but the first thing we must do is order a DNA test to confirm if he is or is not your biological father."

Her eyes came back into focus, as she nodded her head in agreement.

I went out and retrieved a couple of bottles of water to help us focus. Sam and Tyler approached. Sam started with, "Hey who is going to play me when this becomes a movie?"

I was not amused.

Tyler shook his head in the affirmative then chimed in. "Can you believe how mad those other reporters are going to be when they realize the story Sam and I coauthor? It sucks to be banished."

It made me feel better that they were taking a team approach to the reporting of the story. At least my faith in those two was proving to be the right thing. After that encounter I went into the room with Alexandria's family to let them know what was going on.

They were visibly shaken. The bishop gathered them together to pray so I exited the room.

We were going to need DNA samples from Alexandria and Alan to do the test. That meant a continuance in the trial. Everyone in the reporting world waited outside and knew Alexandria was inside the courthouse. They did not know her family was in there and I wanted to keep it that way. They also didn't have a clue about a potential father. I came up with an exit plan.

I asked the bailiff to come into the room with Alexandria and bring an evidence envelope and scissors with him. When he entered, I asked him to cut a sample from Alexandria's hair and seal it up so it could be sent for the DNA test. He signed and dated it for official evidence. I ran my plan by Alexandria, and she agreed with it. We had to get her out of the court- house and back with her family for the foreseeable future. I left her in the room by herself.

When I re-entered the courtroom everyone else was already in their seats. The bailiff once again announced the judge and we were back in session. The judge waved at me, and I stood. "Your Honor, we request a continuance in this case and ask for a court-ordered DNA test to confirm or contest Master Sergeant Johnson's parental claim. My client has already provided a hair sample to the bailiff for the DNA test." The judge looked over to the bailiff who held up the sealed envelope for all to see.

The judge replied, "This case will be continued, and the court orders a DNA test to be completed. This case will be revisited in one week at ten o'clock."

Jeremy's attorney stood and asked to address the court. The judge again acknowledged him."Will the same gag order be in place for the courthouse again next week? There are only two reporters in here today."

The judge asked, "How many do you think we need? Do you not think they will fairly report what has happened here today? Are you not going to hold a press conference as soon as you exit the building?"

Tom Dugan coughed, trying to figure out what to say. Finally, he said, "It's not fair to let these two have the story with no one else able to be in here."

Judge Anthony Richards stood and exclaimed, "I do not care about fair. We are to allow freedom of the press and we have two able-bodied press representatives here today. What I care about is the safety of this town and my courthouse. I will not have it turned into a circus. Bailiff, please make sure the next time we meet the same two reporters are allowed inside the courthouse and no one else." With that he stood and slammed his gavel down hard. "Court is adjourned." The judge walked out leaving Jeremy's attorney dumbfounded.

I looked over at Tyler and Sam in disbelief. I was not entirely sure the judge could banish all the other reporters, but I guess safety concerns jus- tified his response. I was sure Jeremy's attorney would not be challenging the ruling.

TWENTY-FIVE

It was time to leave the courthouse and everyone in the world wanted a photo of Alexandria. I had a plan that I thought would work. I went outside and saw the mob of reporters, who were really whipped up at this point. They had been tricked into banishment and were not happy about it. I wanted to tell them it was their own fault because of the mob scene they had created inside the courthouse but knew they wouldn't see it that way. I had called my assistant, Brenda, and saw her making her way up the side of the crowd. I went outside and the reporters erupted. I went up to the microphone and when they quieted, I told them Jeremy would be out in two minutes to give them a statement. I approached Brenda and everyone saw her give me a bag with a large straw hat poking out.

I went back in, pointed at the reporters and told Jeremy, "They're all yours."

He had his own press conference where he could make the narrative fit any story he wanted. They only thing holding him back was Tyler and Sam who knew what was really said in the courtroom.

Tyler and Sam had formed a journalistic team so Tyler returned to his Airbnb to start the story they would coauthor while Sam stayed to listen to what Jeremy said to the other reporters. If Jeremy made up too much Sam was there to correct the story. When Jeremy opened the courthouse door the reporters erupted in a flurry of questions. Each one shouting to try to get their question answered.

I went inside room eight where Alexandria's family was gathered. I asked Jonathon if they were ready, and he assured me they were. I told him as soon as I drove away from the building a lot of the reporters would follow, clearing the way through the back door. They should be able to leave unnoticed.

I went to room ten and asked Rebecca, "Are you ready for this?"

She looked me in the eye and said, "Yes."

My car was parked in the side lot so she and I left by the side entrance. With her hat pulled down covering her face no one would ever expect that Alexandria and Rebecca had switched clothes and places during the last part of the court proceedings. A reporter saw us approaching my car and yelled questions at us. Jeremy was at the podium but had not spoken yet. Most of the journalists left their camera positions to surround our car. We made it inside and locked the doors, but were completely engulfed in reporters. We were not going anywhere. Two sheriff's deputies tried to intervene, but the world had waited all these months for Alex to appear and would not be denied.

We sat there for a few minutes. I was relieved when I saw two Amish buggies turn the corner about a block away and slowly move down the road. I looked at Rebecca. "This is as far ahead as I had planned. Any suggestions at this point?"

She smiled and instructed, "Yes, I do. Pull out of the parking lot slowly and head down Main Street."

Since I didn't have a better plan or any plan at all, I put the car in drive and honked the horn. I eased out of the parking lot and onto Main Street. Many people ran beside our car while some went back to their vehicles and followed. A lot of photographers attempted to get photos as we moved along slowly. About two blocks in we approached the traffic light.

Rebecca divulged the next part of her idea. "I want you to purposely stop at the green light. As it turns yellow, hit the gas and go through."

I didn't have time to think ahead, so I obeyed. As the light turned yellow, I hit the gas, at that same time I realized there were buggies at the intersection ready to cross. We slipped through just ahead of six buggies, three in each lane, that crossed in front of the cars following us. The reporters honked their horns to encourage the Amish to move their buggies.

When the honking started all the horses stopped dead in their tracks. It was total grid lock behind us as we drove away.

Rebecca once again gave instructions. "Speed up for three blocks then take a left. Stop at the next buggy you see. I will jump out and get in with them."

"There is a flaw in your plan," I exclaimed, "You're dressed in Alexandria's clothes. They might not recognize you."

She smiled at me and said, "Do you really think anyone in the Amish community does not know about Alexandria and her being with my family. All those children that left on rumspringa and never returned? She is the first modern child to convert to our way of life. News of her conversion is probably known nationwide in our faith."

It hit me that all those people knew where she was and not one had taken up Jeremy's $50,000 reward. What a testament to their community. As I rounded the corner after three blocks, I saw a buggy heading the same way as us.

Rebecca said, "There, drop me off right in front of them and make your get away. The next reporter that sees you will not see Alexandria." She was taking a leap of faith.

I stopped ten feet in front of the buggy. She jumped out and yelled, "GO."

I pulled away. I looked in my rearview mirror as the buggy came to a stop and saw her motioning as she explained what was happening. Then I saw a hand reach down to pull her up into the carriage. She was gone.

As I drove away, I was astounded at what the family had just pulled off. Somehow, they had gotten four other buggies to join them in the traffic jam. One of the older boys must have slipped out while I was with Rebecca. I chuckled thinking of all those reporters trying to find Alexandria and I was sure she was in one of those buggies blocking traffic.

I took the next right and sped up to the speed limit. About four minutes later a car pulled up beside me and looked in. The only thing they saw was me driving alone in my car. They continued to follow, so I decided to take a little road trip. After about thirty minutes I headed back into town. By then I had four vehicles following me. They must have called each other on their cell phones. I pulled up in front of the police station, got out of my car and went inside. Several reporters yelled questions at me. I ignored them all. Even though it was a public building none of the horde ventured in. The car was swarmed and examined to make sure Alexandria wasn't hiding inside.

The chief of police stood by the window, watching my car being searched. "Are you ready to surrender or seeking sanctuary?"

I went over to the coffee pot and started to pour a cup. "Can it be both or do I have to choose?" I finished pouring and went over and sat in the chair by his desk. "Can I just sit here a little while? I want to figure out my next move."

The chief came over and sat in his official chair behind the desk and said, "As much trouble and chaos as you brought to our town, I should probably put you on a three-day psychiatric hold."

The thought of three days in a quiet room without a computer or talking to anyone was compelling. He let me sit for a minute in quiet while I drank my coffee, then I realized he was just sitting here with me while his town was out of control. I finally sat up and asked, "Shouldn't you be somewhere? I mean the town is swamped by reporters right now."

He sat back in his chair and smiled. "That's what I have deputies for. But now that you mention it, I need to go outside and talk to a few fellows loitering in front of the station." I took the cue and swallowed the last of the coffee.

The chief went out first and told the four guys to follow him to his car. They walked over to him. As I exited the building, I heard him giving them the definition of loitering and how standing in front of a police station was suspicious. I also heard one of the reporters explain they were just waiting outside for me. To this the chief responded, "Well, then let me tell you what the penalties and fines are for harassment and stalking." I drove away thinking how nice it was to live in a small town while the four were held captive by the chief

There were so many cars parked around my office, I had to park a block away. It had been over an hour since I left the courthouse, so I figured Jeremy's press conference was over. The world would finally have the real news on what was happening with the internet star's life.

Sam and Tyler's firsthand account of the story would make the biggest splash, but Jeremy's press conference was also covered. Tyler had gotten the farewell story from Alexandria. The other reporters home offices had contacted Tyler's editor about running his story, for a fee of course. I am sure there was a lot of money made by Tyler's home paper. As I approached my office I was recognized. About ten reporters surrounded me and yelled questions in my direction. I pushed through without saying a word, closed and locked the door behind me while flipping the CLOSED sign in place.

Brenda was at her desk. The phone rang and she answered it. I knew it was probably a reporter wanting an interview. Assistants like her are hard to find. She watches over the office and protects me from unwanted phone calls or meetings. Without asking, she politely told the caller that she would take their name and number but, unfortunately, I was unavailable right now and the office was closed for the rest of the day. She jotted down their name and number and hung up the phone. I saw her add the phone message to a growing pile. Then she handed me the stack. I took a quick glance at the ten to twelve messages, held them up and asked, "Do I need to answer any of these?" She shook her head no.

I filled her in on what had transpired in the courtroom. She had already seen a news clip about the long-lost father being found. "Is it true?" she asked.

"Maybe," was the only answer I had. The fact that Alexandria could have a father changes the emancipation proceeding. A potential legal guardian coming forward at this point would have to be considered in the well-being of the minor. I needed to interview him. He could be a good guy that Alexandria needs to get to know. I knew she loved her new family but if the test proves he is her father, then she should give him a chance.

"Get me Jeremy's phone number." As I dialed, I knew he would be smirking when he answered the call. For now, he had bested me, and I had to accept that. My call was forwarded to his cell phone, and he answered immediately.

He must have had me as a saved contact because when he answered, he said, "Counselor, I've been waiting for your call." He was savoring the moment.

I hated that he had won the round, but I needed to concentrate on the task at hand. To sound professional, I answered with, "Mr. Staley, I would like to set up a meeting with Master Sergeant Johnson. I'm hoping we can meet in person, if he is still in town."

Jeremy answered, "Absolutely, when do you have time?"

"I've cleared my schedule and hope we can get together this afternoon." We agreed on 1:00 P.M.

Brenda had already googled Alan Johnson and found some preliminary information. Everything looked pretty basic. He had entered the military at age nineteen and served overseas on four tours during the Second Gulf War. He was a 46S communications specialist. He had been in the army approximately seventeen years and had advanced through the ranks. He was now a master sergeant based at Fort Dix, New Jersey. I read up on the job duties of a communications specialist in the Army and found his job entailed researching and distributing news releases and photographs of Army personnel and activities. In other words, he's a reporter for the Army.

This meant he was intelligent. He had served with distinction in his duties. On paper he looked to be the real deal. A father that never knew he had a daughter. I was hoping the interview would give me some evidence one way or the other on Master Sergeant Alan Johnson.

At 1:00 P.M. someone jiggled then tapped on the door of our office. Brenda opened it carefully, making sure it was Johnson. Much to the dismay of four reporters still waiting outside, he was allowed in while they continued to wait. She led him to the conference room where he took a seat. I heard her offer him coffee and he accepted. I waited a few minutes to figure out what I was going to ask this man. After failing to come up with a strategy, I figured I had kept him waiting long enough. I would have to wing it.

As I approached, he stood to shake my hand. Sitting across from each other I knew I had to guide the interview. "Sergeant Johnson, I am sure you are aware how hard this is for me. I'm trying to do the best I can for Alexandria and what she wants done. We will need the DNA test back to confirm you're her father. If it comes back positive and you are her father, I want to know what your plans are. Where will you live? Where you will work?...those kinds of things. You must realize Alexandria doesn't know you and now she is faced with a possible long-lost father." He sat quietly as I spoke.

When I finished, he looked at me and stated, "If Alex is my daughter, I want to become the father I should have been all these years. I never knew she existed. I'm willing to drop everything to start a new life with her."

"That sounds good but what about your military career?"

"I wouldn't have a problem transferring to a reserve unit and working out of their facility for the remaining three years until I have enough service time to retire.

"Where would you live?" I asked.

"There's a reserve unit near Jeremy. We would buy a home near the area so Alex would feel comfortable."

"How do you feel about Alexandria not continuing on Jeremy's internet shows?"

He lowered his head for the first time and looked away. "We'll have to talk about that."

At that point I knew he was a gold digger. I asked about his personal finances, and he shrugged his shoulders. "Are you aware that Alexandria instructed me to give all her money to charity?"

He sat up straight and exclaimed, "As her father and legal guardian I will oversee her money." So, there it was. Plain and simple. He was after her money. He didn't care about her at all.

I was furious. This man was just another of Jeremy's pawns. He didn't care about Alexandria. I stood from the table. "This meeting is over." I picked up my tablet and walked out of the room.

As I left, he shouted, "When it comes back that I'm her father you'll have no legal way to stop me from exerting my parental rights. I did not abandon her. I still have my rights as her father." He had obviously been talking to Jeremy's attorney. As sad as it sounds, he was probably right.

Brenda escorted him out. I had some serious research to do on the subject.

Twenty-Six

My research failed to find clear cases that applied to Alexandria's situation. I preferred being the one arguing the father had parental rights. It only makes sense the father has rights to guardianship. But on the other hand, she was filing for emancipation so she could run her own life. That had not changed. There is no reason to force her to go with a father she didn't know. As an emancipated adult, she can choose to seek a relationship with her father if she wants. I wondered, *If she didn't have any money would her so-called father be so anxious to drop everything to be her guardian.* I don't want to judge him, but the fact there was so much money involved made his motivation suspect. We would just have to wait and see.

Two days later, I received a letter from the court informing me that Mr. Johnson was in fact her biological father. My heart sank. Before this unforeseen issue I was confident the judge would grant her petition of emancipation. I wasn't sure how Jeremy had found this man, but DNA doesn't lie. Even though she doesn't know him, the court will be inclined to grant custody to her father. The fact he was unaware of her existence will play in his favor. I had to get a message to Alexandria so she could prepare for what could be an unwanted outcome of her court proceedings.

I went to the fruit and vegetable stand but did not see her or Jonathon. An elderly lady took my list, opened it and started reading. Without hesitation she turned and went in the back and packed my would-be order. I wondered how many of the Amish community were in on this. When

162

she finished, she brought up my bag and said, "That will be $12 right now. The rest of what you wanted will be at your place at 5:00 A.M. tomorrow. "I paid her $15 and told her to keep the change. Without even looking at me, she put the money in the cash bag she carried and walked away. Just one more customer for the day. I looked in the bag and saw an assortment of vegetables. Thank God not a piece of fruit in sight. I know the Amish are early risers and we wanted to keep Alexandria out of the reporters' grasp, but I'm getting tired of these early morning meetings.

News had been leaked that Alexandria's long-lost father had been found. Jeremy had issued a statement that he was happy for Alex and was looking forward to working with the new family in the future. He had declared victory in the case and expected me to accept defeat. I had to find a way to help Alexandria. Attacking Master Sergeant Johnson's character would be tough. The fact that he showed up at the last minute was not reason enough to dismiss his claim to guardianship. He was Alexandria's father. He could and should have some parental rights.

Reporters were still following me pretty much everywhere, but they knew my routine was to leave my house at 8:00 A.M. and go to the diner for breakfast, meaning they didn't show up at my house until 7:30. So I wasn't surprised that no one was around when I left at 4:45 A.M. The streets were completely empty as I drove to my office in the dark. When I arrived at 4:50 I turned on the lights and waited for Alexandria.

Not sixty seconds later, the door opened and Alexandria and Jonathon walked in. They headed directly to the conference room. I followed and sat down across from them. I didn't know how to tell Alexandria that Alan Johnson was her real father. How could I tell her that I had no plan to challenge his claim to parental rights? It's not like he was a bad father, he had no knowledge of her existence. As I looked into her ever so innocent eyes, I hesitated. Finally, I decided the best way was to just come out with it. "Alexandria," I said, "The DNA test came back, and confirms that Master Sergeant Alan Johnson is your biological father."

She put her hand to her mouth and lowered her head. She was devastated. I thought she was going to burst into tears. I was ready for the worst.

I was shocked when Jonathon said, "Oh stop it. We do not have time for all of this."

Then, with a grin on her face Alexandria looked at me and said, "We heard through the grapevine that it was on the news last night."

I had stayed up late struggling with how to tell her and she already knew it. On top of it all she was messing with me, making me relieved and furious at the same time.

I decided to hit her head on with it. "I do not believe we will win your emancipation case. Your father has a perfect military record and since he didn't know about you, he couldn't have abandoned you, meaning he still retains parental rights under the law. I interviewed him, and he seemed like a decent guy, but he intends on living close to Jeremy and wants you to continue the internet shows. He is also under the impression that he can seize control of your money once he is named your guardian."

Her grin vanished in an instant. She sat up in her chair and calmly said, "Please keep trying to find a way to stop him from becoming my legal guardian. If you cannot, I assure you I will not live with him."

I tried to explain the court would decide whether she could be emancipated or her father be her guardian.

She stood and said, "Just do your best to make it happen, I will see you at the next court date." With that said, she and Johnathon walked out the door.

As I sat at the conference desk, I felt like her whole future was resting in my hands. When I looked down, I noticed an envelope sitting in the middle of the desk. Alexandria must have dropped it when she left. My heart stopped as I opened it and saw Mark's letterhead on the top. All it said was,

You got this, buddy. Alexandria needs you. You're almost there.

I tried to comprehend when he could have written this. Did Mark even know about Alan Johnson? Did he realize I was probably going to lose this case and her father would have guardianship over her? I ran outside to catch Alexandria to get an explanation about the letter. As I reached the sidewalk, I saw Alexandria and Jonathon rounding the corner a block ahead. I stopped dead in my tracks when I saw Alexandria holding something next to her ear. *She was talking to someone on a cell phone.* My mind went in ten different directions as I tried to comprehend what I saw. Cell phones were forbidden in her new world but there it was clear as day. There was no way to explain it away. All this cloak and dagger stuff with the Amish fruit stand and all she had to do was call me. My brain moved to the dark side, and I started imagining that I was being played the whole time.

I forgot about chasing them down and just went back inside. It was too early to call Mark, but I planned to call as soon as I could. Other than his letters, I had not heard a word from him. He did not answer or return my phone calls or return my emails. It was frustrating. He had brought me this case and left me to struggle through alone. Suddenly, a calm came over me when I realized what Mark had written was correct. I was almost there. The case should be decided next week. No matter what happens the end was near. Worst case scenario was that Alexandria isn't granted her request for emancipation and her father becomes her guardian. Either way it ends for me. Whatever game is being played out will be over soon.

The next few days were spent digging into cases involving long-lost fathers coming back for guardianship. No matter what was happening with Alexandria and her cell phone, I still wanted to try my best. This case would end soon and so would my opportunity to bill her for my hours.

I emailed and called Mark but as usual received no response. I was on my own.

Jeremy was on the news a lot over the next few days telling everyone about Alex's return to the show. He promised new adventures to their followers. I could only imagine how many new subscribers had signed up since all this began. Hard to believe that Alexandria had not been seen in over four months and still her followers remained faithful. The money in her account had probably doubled by now. And Jeremy kept ninety percent. *What a cash cow he had created.*

I continued going over case law, but couldn't come up with anything I thought would sway the judge. Everything was in place for her emancipation until her father came into the picture. I had no smoking gun, as they say, to nullify Alan Johnson's claim to guardianship. All I could do was present the facts and let the judge decide.

Alexandria having a cell phone still bothered me. Plus, Jonathon was right beside her in an obvious acceptance of her actions. The Amish are not allowed electronics, not to mention how did she keep it charged. No electricity on the homestead would create a problem. Who was she calling? What were they talking about? I was looking forward to all this being over.

TWENTY-SEVEN

What should be the last day of the case finally arrived. Alexandria knew what time to arrive, so I didn't worry about her. I arrived at the courthouse an hour early to find hundreds of news people gathered on the courthouse steps. Extra deputies were brought in for crowd control. Most of the spectators had gotten accustomed to staying outside but a few still tried to argue for their right to be inside the courthouse. They were quickly told they could wait out front or be escorted off the property.

Since Sam and Tyler were still the only two reporters allowed in the building again today, they took the classy route and arrived at the back door to avoid being seen, and were let in by a security guard expecting them. I saw them in the outer hall and stopped to chat. Both had done a few interviews on television, which triggered my greeting. "Since I am in the presence of television stars should I kneel or bow?"

Tyler looked at Sam and asked, "I prefer him kneeling, but will leave it up to you."

Sam raised his hand to his cheek like he was pondering something and then waved his hand and announced, "A simple bow will do." Tyler nodded in agreement.

I did a half bow towards both, and they stuck out their hands to be shook. We had all experienced a wild ride this last month, but it was about to be over. After some small talk they asked how I thought it would go? I shook my head. "I might as well get use to saying it. The facts are the facts. There just isn't a good way to impeach the father's claim." They both nodded their heads in agreement.

I decided to check on Alexandria expecting she and her family would be in the conference room again, but when I knocked and peeked in no one was in there. I checked all the conference rooms, but they were empty. How was she going to get into the courthouse without being seen? If she didn't show up, she would be in contempt of court. If they asked me where she was, I honestly wouldn't know where to start. The people who placed her there would know. Then I remembered one of Mark's early letters said something about trying to keep any of us from going to jail. Was she planning on running away? She could travel to another state with other Amish families and never be found. The facts were simple. She loved her Amish family and she only had about sixteen months before she turned eighteen and became a legal adult. *Running away did not make sense.*

Thirty minutes before our scheduled court appearance, I heard someone blasting a car horn followed by screams and shouts. I exited the building through the front door and stood on the now empty courthouse steps. Everyone was running toward the noise. I gasped at the stretch limousine sitting in the middle of the street. Standing through the open sunroof was Alexandria. She waved at the crowd of reporters and fans surrounding the car. I couldn't believe it. She went from hiding in the shadows to full transparency. It was Alexandria, but then again it wasn't. Her hair was blond but teased up in the front and sides. As she turned, I saw the back was purple. She wore big hoop earrings and a nose ring hung down to her lip. She jumped up on the top of the car and swirled around to give the fans a complete look at her outfit. A tight, low-cut, cropped tank top showed her midriff and barely-there cutoff shorts. Looking closer, I saw tattoos running up and down her arms as well as on her legs. The final touch was the tongue piercing she flaunted by sticking out her tongue to show the crowd.

Watching in utter amazement, I realized this was not the Alexandria Andres I knew and represented. The crowd chanted, "ALEX, ALEX, ALEX."

I had skimmed a few of the Alex videos but never really paid close attention to the character she was playing. Alex was over the top.

She played to her fans, kicking her legs high and blowing kisses. As she walked down the hood of the car, people waited to help her down. Instead of jumping down, however, she turned and raised her hands over her head. The crowd erupted as she arched her back stiff and fell backwards into the crowd. They closed in and caught her. I had heard of crowd surfing but had never seen it in person. The crowd held her in the air as she floated ten feet one way then ten feet back and around the crowd. This lasted about a minute until she relaxed her back and was lowered by a couple of fans. She jumped up and down with her hands clapping up in the air. The chant started again. "ALEX, ALEX, ALEX."

Having seen enough I went back inside the courthouse. Everyone in the street was getting high on their favorite drug. The fans had waited a long time and their queen had finally returned. It was pandemonium.

I began to wonder if this whole thing was a sham from the beginning. The girl was a great actor. Could she have a split personality? What was her true end game? In thirty minutes, we'll have the judge's verdict. I looked down the block toward the Amish fruit and vegetable stand. It was gone. I wondered if they all knew Alex was going to appear, and they didn't want anything to do with her.

Jeremy and company must be thrilled. Not only had Alex returned she had done so in spectacular form. *How many more subscribers had she just acquired,* I wondered.

I walked by Tyler and Sam staring out the window at the bedlam a few feet away. They, too, were amazed at what they saw. Tyler smirked as he said, "Well, at least you know she showed up."

I never broke stride and never looked at him. I walked straight into the courtroom where the bailiff sat. He asked me what was going on out there. I just shook my head and said, "You do not want to know."

At five minutes before court was supposed to be in session, everyone was in their places and seated except Alex. She arrived with two minutes to spare. She took her seat beside me. I didn't know what to say. This is not the girl I agreed to represent. What was going on?

The bailiff instructed us to stand as the judge entered and I saw the shock on his face as he looked at Alex sitting beside me. The clerk called the case number, and we were directed to sit. The judge kept starring at Alex as he spoke. He talked about the DNA findings, and the importance the court places on family ties and unity. We all knew where this was going. He was about to grant Alan Johnson guardianship over Alexandria.

As he continued, Alex took out a piece of bubble gum and started chewing, smacking her lips loudly and blowing an occasional bubble for good measure. The judge was so confused he stopped speaking. He then asked, "Stand up, Miss Andres. Do you really think it is appropriate to chew gum in my courtroom?"

She removed the gum from her mouth and defiantly stuck it under the table. Judge Richards' rage was unmistakable as he stared at Alex. Without further prompting she reached under the table and retrieved the gum. She pulled the wrapper from out of her pocket and placed the gum in it. The judge's shoulders visibly relaxed as Alex wadded it up in a ball. Then as if on cue and in an overly exaggerated move, she extended her arm out over the aisle and dropped the garbage on the floor.

The judge immediately stood and instructed her to pick up her trash. She stared back at him. As a further act of defiance, she crossed her arms in front of her. The judge's face turned red. No one had ever been so disrespectful in his courtroom. In a calm voice he said, "You will pick that up or I will fine you for littering."

Alex's arms remained crossed and her stare intensified. She raised one eyebrow and asked, "How much is a littering fine?"

The judge turned to the bailiff who said, "$50."

Alex smirked and exclaimed, "Let's make it $100 and I'll just leave it there."

I reached for Alexandria's arm to have a word with her, but she pulled away. I quickly stood, asking the judge for a brief recess.

He looked at me and said, "No."

I sat back down.

The judge was furious at the lack of respect being shown in his courtroom. He ordered Alex to have a seat. She remained standing with her arms crossed. Alex's belligerence had pushed Judge Richards' buttons as his infuriation with her grew. "Young lady, if you do not sit down right now, I will find you in contempt of court and fine you $500."

Alex threw her head back and laughed. "How about I skip the apology and pay $1,000?"

The judge realized the money angle was lost on her, so he decided on a different approach. He grabbed his gavel and said, "Fine, the city will take your $1,000 and I'll raise you one night in county jail. Let's see if that changes your attitude. Bailiff, take her away." With that he slammed down his gavel, stepped off the bench and went back into his chambers.

The bailiff approached Alex, placing his hand on her elbow to lead her away. I expected her to resist but she didn't. He led her out the back door. The clerk announced court would reconvene at 10:00 A.M. tomorrow. I was stunned. Alex had showed up and caused utter chaos in the courtroom. She had certainly squashed any chance of her being emancipated. I truly believed the judge was about to grant legal guardianship to Alan Johnson. The chaos of today only postponed the inevitable ruling until tomorrow. Now, Alex looked forward to a night in jail. I hope it'll do some good, but I doubted it.

Twenty-Eight

I left the courthouse through the side door to avoid the fans and reporters still gathered out front. Alex's photo would be shared across thousands of newspapers, broadcast channels, and other media outlets in the next few hours. Walking quickly, I made it back to my office before news of what happened inside the courtroom filtered out to the masses on the street.

Brenda and I discussed everything leading up to Alex's appearance. We tried to figure out how her temper tantrum, for lack of better description, could be turned so it played in her favor. Maybe, she just felt like she had lost complete control of her life and went berserk. Booking her would take some time, so I waited at my office. The phone rang incessantly, and each time Brenda brushed off reporters begging for a statement.

A few minutes later, she appeared at my door. "There's a reporter here to see you."

"The last thing I want right now is see a reporter."

Then from the outer office, someone said, "What if I bring a fruit basket as a bribe?" Recognizing Tyler's voice, I motioned for her to let him in.

He came in smiling. "How many copies of tonight's late edition do you want?" Tyler sat down, across from me and asked the obvious. "What's up with your client, now?"

All I could do was shrug my shoulders. I looked at him and said, "You're the super sleuth. What do you make of it?" His shoulders went up and down.

We agreed emancipation left the realm of possibilities once her father had shown up, but we couldn't understand her sudden act of defiance or how it could possibly help. Now, she had to sit in jail for the night.

Tyler was hoping to get something from me but realized I was still trying to wrap my head around it. We talked for a few minutes, then he excused himself since he had another big story to write.

I figured I had allowed enough time for Alex to be booked and headed over to the jail to consult with my client. After checking in at the front desk, I was shown to a conference room and told she would be brought in shortly. She was escorted to the room within five minutes. Having been sentenced to only a one-day incarceration, she was still dressed in the same clothes she had worn to court.

She sat down across the table from me. "I know you don't understand, but I want to make one thing clear. I will not go home with Jeremy or my father as my guardian."

"That's not a decision that you, or I, can make. It's completely up to the judge."

She was calm and cool when she got up and said, "Wait and see." With that said she walked over and banged on the door. The guard opened the door, and she walked away. I had no idea what was going on.

I returned to the office hoping to find something in case law that could help. There was nothing new. My mind was tired but wouldn't shut off. I still couldn't get over how a change of clothing and a little extra make-up turned one person into another. She was two completely different people. One clean and wholesome and one totally wild. Jeremy had created two totally different personas and pitted them against each other on the internet. He was the first person to accomplish this and no one else had been able to successfully copy it. What would have become of this young woman if she had never met Jeremy.

I walked into the courthouse at 9:00 A.M. An hour before court was to reconvene. The crowd had easily doubled in size from yesterday. Alex's fans and the reporters hoped for a repeat of what they had witnessed the day before, but I knew they would bring her through the back like any other prisoner.

I was her attorney. She had called me her champion. Yet, I had no plan as to what to say. How had this simple case gone so sideways? I knew Alex wouldn't be brought in until the case was called so I went in and sat at my appointed chair.

Jeremy and company were already inside. He boldly came up to me and asked, "What are you trying to pull?"

I looked at him and honestly said, "I have no clue what is happening."

Apparently, he didn't like my answer because he kind of snorted and walked away.

Exactly at 10:00 A.M. we all stood as the judge entered. He instructed us to sit. As the case number was read the door opened and in walked Alex escorted by a deputy. She was seated beside me as the court clerk finished reading the documents. The judge began by saying he was here to rule on the guardianship of the minor Alexandria Andres, but first we had unfinished business from yesterday. With a loud stern voice he said, "Miss Andres, after spending a night in our jail do you have anything to say to the court?"

I prayed that she had come to her senses.

She calmy stood and said, "Your Honor, I want to go on the record as saying I will not go home with Jeremy or Master Sergeant Johnson as my guardian." With that said, she once again defiantly folded her arms across her chest.

The judge's face immediately took a crimson hue. The courtroom was dead silent. He said, "I want an apology for your behavior, or I will continue my contempt order and give you ten days in jail."

Arms still folded across her chest, she responded, "Well, you're not going to get it so let's not waste time. Let's go for thirty days."

The judge's anger increased as his voice grew louder. Taking a deep breath in an effort to calm himself, he continued. "Since you like being locked up I'm sending you back to that work camp so you won't be able to just sit around and relax."

Suddenly, I got it. Alexandria was all in on the bluff of her lifetime. She would either win big or lose big.

The judge continued, "And since you don't have any aversion to spending money, I am also ordering that you pay the $1,000 per month the county would normally pay the work farm for keeping you. What do you have to say to that?"

Alex unclasped her arms, letting them fall to her sides. It looked like the judge had broken her and she buckled. Then she looked him straight in the eye and said, "Well, I am kind of a pain in the butt, so let's make it $2,000 a month.

The judge said, "Fine. You will be remanded to the work farm for thirty days. You will pay the $2,000 room and board. We'll revisit this case in thirty days where you will give a heartfelt apology to this court, or be returned to the detention farm. I want to also add that if you attempt to run away from your detention center you still have a three-year jail sentence that would come into effect." Alex lowered her head.

Jeremy's attorney, Tom Dugan, raised his hand to be recognized. The judge motioned him to speak. Clearing his throat he asked, "What about the guardianship decision?"

The judge leaned forward. "Because she'll remain in the state's custody, I'm appointing a temporary guardian for the court. Guardian *ad litem* for the minor Alexandria Andres is her attorney. We will continue the case for her permanent guardianship when she apologizes to the court and her contempt order is cancelled. I expect to see you all in thirty days when we can get this resolved."

I looked up at Alexandria and softly said, "Or maybe not."

The judge banged the gavel, stood and walked out.

The bailiff took Alexandria by the arm to escort her out the back. I asked if I could have a minute with my client and he pointed towards the back, so I followed them out. He took us to one of the conference rooms and left us alone.

When the door closed Alexandria threw her arms around me and hugged me tightly then realized what she was doing and stepped back. We stood there looking at each other and I finally asked, "Did we win or lose?"

"It depends on whether the judge is a man of his word or not. For the next sixteen months I will not be apologizing. If he keeps his word, I will stay with my work family until I am eighteen. Then I'll be my own guardian. Hopefully, Jeremy and his squad will give up, but I doubt it."

"As much as I wish otherwise, I'm afraid you're right."

I quickly learned that my client wasn't giving up either, as she went on to explain something else on her mind.

"I have come up with a plan to throw them off their game. They say the best defense is a good offense. I want you, as my attorney, to have an audit conducted of all the money that has come in since my online programs began. My contract says I get ten percent of the gross revenues. Not the net revenue after expenses. My grandmother was sharp to have added that phrase into the contract. No one has questioned Jeremy's bookkeeping in the last four years. Have one of those big accounting firms crawl up every nook and cranny. Threaten an IRS audit if he gives you problems. It is not a question of whether he embezzled money, it's how much. The websites and chat rooms should generate income for years. I don't want or need the money, but I don't want him to get it. We will find a way to distribute it to help people we want it to go to. I hope you are up to managing my affairs for the long term. Will you continue to fight the good fight for me?"

Yesterday, I thought this would be all over and we would part ways. Today, she was asking me to be linked to her permanently. I stuck out my hand but before we shook, I said, "There is only one condition. I don't ever want to be involved with ALEX ever again."

She grabbed my hand and smiled. "No guarantees."

Before I released her hand, I had to ask, "What's up with the cell phone I saw you using?"

"It was gift from Judge Mark so we could stay in touch through all this." She pulled her hand back and smiled. "It came with a solar charger so I don't need electricity."

"But what about the Amish restrictions?"

She explained the bishop had granted a special circumstance exception since nothing like this had ever happened before. She gave me her number and instructed me that she only turns it on at 6:00 A.M. each day to check messages. If I needed her, I should leave a text message and she would see it the next morning.

I still didn't know where she was living, but I didn't really need to know. Plenty of reporters were still looking for her and sometimes ignorance truly is bliss

The deputy knocked on the door and peeked in. I motioned that we were done. He opened the door all the way and out she went. I would see Alexandria many times after this, but I prayed it was the last time I would ever see Alex.

The next day I received a call from Mark congratulating me on the job I had done. After ranting at him for getting me into all of this, I finally gave him a chance to defend himself.

He responded with simple questions. "Did you go to jail? Get hurt or die?"

"No, I did not die or go to jail...but I could have." At that point, I couldn't help but smile. "You should have seen those Alex fans. They went wild."

For a few seconds I heard nothing but silence, then he said, "You're right, they were wild. Jonathon and I saw the whole thing from the back of the limo."

It all fell into place that Mark had been guiding Alexandria through this whole case. Was the whole thing a set up? Alex disrespecting the judge certainly looked real. I knew it was better not to ask questions I might not want answered.

Since I had not died, I thanked him for giving me this case. My life has been completely turned upside down, and I was forever grateful.

www.ingramcontent.com/pod-product-compliance
Lightning Source LLC
Chambersburg PA
CBHW050941120626
46552CB00001B/316